The Wicked Heart

GRAVES Book One

R.C. Rodriguez

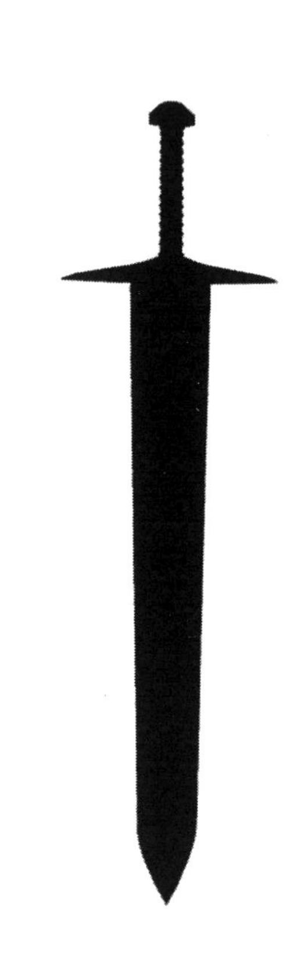

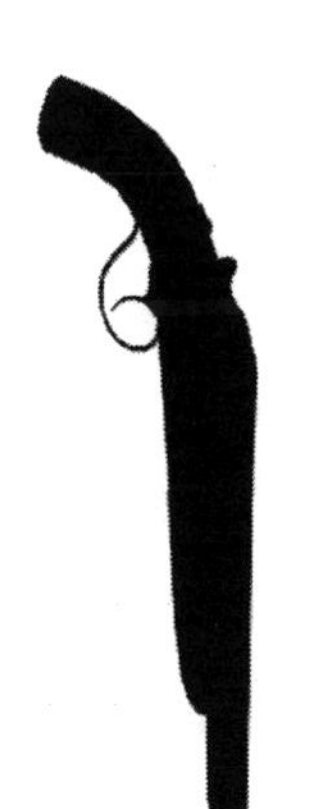

ISBN-13: 9798521359042

To my friends who read my stuff, and my parents who made it possible.

Contents

Chapter 1

Listings

Playground swingset swinging by itself. Really loud.

My eyes burned as I blinked away the pooling moisture. They stung from hours staring at my computer screen; this had to be the 300th job listing I'd read that morning. And it was about a fucking swingset.

The mouse wheel clicked as I scrolled, not hopeful in the slightest.

I keep hearing moaning coming from my bedroom, especially when I'm not in it.

Sounds less like a vengeful spook, I thought, *and more like a lonely wife. I guess I could help the guy out, but it ain't ghost hunting.*

I kept reading.

The government is putting fluoride in the drinking water. Beware.

My fingers dug into my skin as I pinched between my brows, a rattling sigh making my lips flap.

The Union really let any stupid fuck post on their site. I mean, that last one wasn't even about ghosts! *How am I supposed to further my career as hunter if these idiots are posting about...* I read the next listing... *fucking chemtrails! Jesus!*

Something lithe and sleek rubbed against my bare leg: my black cat, Hans. He mewed at me, so I leaned down and gave him a scratch on the forehead, much to his purring pleasure. The cat plopped next to his empty food dish, staring at me with feline slits. Sighing, I stood and stretched, cool autumn wind drafting underneath my shack's door and brushing my moist bare skin.

My forest shack was a little more than dilapidated. I'd stumbled upon when I'd first... *moved* here, and had done little in terms of home improvement. The roof was missing some of its metal sheets, letting in beams of sunlight dimmed by the encroaching clouds. There was little furniture, but what was there was covered in dust, bugs, and hasty patch-jobs. But, shit, my couch was comfy. What else can a man ask for?

A rat scurried across the concrete floor, sharp nails scritching as he sprinted towards his den. I stared lethargically at it. Hans did the same.

"You could help out with those guys, you know," I said to the cat. His black tail lifted and fell impatiently. I rolled my eyes and went to grab him some slop, crunching some empty beer cans with my bare feet.

Other than Hans' chow, my cabinets were almost empty. There were a few opened Pop-Tarts, a loaf of stale bread, and three lukewarm beers. Oh, and some cobwebs.

This can't go on. I need some fuckin' cash, and fast.

Hans purred gratefully when I plopped the can-shaped food into his bowl. He blinked at me, then returned to his windowsill to sleep the rest of the day away.

Eyelids heavy, I stared at him ruefully. *If only...*

But I had work to do. Those ghosts weren't gonna hunt themselves.

When I returned to my computer, there was a new listing added to the myriad in front of me. *POSSESSION*, it read in giant lettering.

That's more fuckin' like it.

My heartbeat ticked up a few notches with my excitement. It had been a few days since my last gig, which had not gone well. I'd finally get a chance to...

Ah, shit. That *was* my last job.

A guy named Josephi Hostephony had set me up with an easy gig: Old woman possessed and dangerous, and in desperate need of help. Well, I showed up at the Garcias' place with my sword and shotgun, hungry to do some killing... and maybe I'd scared them a little.

In hindsight, "I'll cut her damn head off" is not the best way to console a worried grandson.

I lost the gig before even drawing my sword, and now I owed Josephi Hostephony a fat sum of dough. That was how he rolled: Secure pricy jobs, then dole them out to hunters while taking a cut of the pay despite doing jack shit.

Maybe I oughta serve him back his own nuts as payment, I thought, grinding my teeth.

Knowing that asshole, though, he'd find a way to sell 'em.

According to the Union website, the job had been taken over by a group called the Specter Detectors, a buncha dweebish teenagers no doubt desperate to prove their worth. And here I was, sitting alone and in my underwear, reading about fluoride in the fucking water. I shook my head and shut the computer off.

My front door rattled as someone rapped their knuckles against it. I stood abruptly, the office chair crashing to the ground. This was the first visitor I'd gotten in the months I'd lived in Hartsville. I smelled bad news.

The hinges screamed when I swung the door open, and I came face-to-face with a lovely ray of blonde and black sunshine. The woman was wearing horn-rimmed black glasses, matching her black coat and black skirt. Her lips were painted a cherry-red, her hair was shaved gold, her eyes bluer than the sea.

I know how this went. Damsel in distress shows up at the detective's office hoping for help, pleading and promising that she'll do anything if I — the brilliant, dark, and smoldering detective — aid her in her time of need. I'd solve the case and get some ass to boot. A tale as old as time.

"Are you Mr. Graves?" Her voice was stern and confident.

"Just Graves," I said. "How can I help you, Ms...?"

Ignoring my inferred question, the blonde dug into the black satchel strapped around her shoulder. She whipped out a pair of manila envelopes and handed them to me, face plain and red lips flat. Raising an eyebrow, I grabbed the papers and opened the first.

Mallery Jacobs, 76, has been haunted for the past few weeks. She believes that her husband has been leaving her messages, but I have my doubts judging by letters written in blood. Investigation is required.

A sizeable pay was listed underneath the job description. I nodded, pleased.

"So, what, is Mallery Jacobs your grandma or something?" I asked the blonde. "Why me?"

"Please open the other envelope, Graves."

I did so.

It was a bill from Josephi Hostephony. Fuck.

"You have been ignoring our phone calls for days. Your contract with Mr. Hostephony requires that you pay your debt in full within a week of starting your assigned job, regardless of the outcome." She pushed up her glasses primly. "If you fail to do so, Mr. Hostephony will be forced to report you to the Union, resulting in the very timely revoking of your hunting license."

"Here I thought I was getting some ass," I mumbled.

"Excuse me?"

"I said, this pay isn't even *half* of what I owe that fucking conman. How the hell am I supposed to come up with the rest?"

"That is not our business."

"Yeah, your business is ripping off stupid fucks like me until we're enslaved."

Her stare was cold as ice. "I would recommend haste, Graves. Josephi is not a forgiving man."

"You tell that asshole that I'll give him his fuckin' money," I said, my mouth twisting, "alongside a fist right down his goddamn throat."

"Is that all?" she asked, unphased.

"No. Tell him that, next time he wants to collect a debt from Graves, he'd better come himself. And he'd better bring a fuckin' *army*."

The woman pushed up her glasses again, blue eyes expressionless and apathetic. Without another word, she turned and walked towards her sleek black car, hips swaying subtly and heels leaving little holes in the gravel around my shack.

"God*damnit*," I shouted, slamming the door shut. "Not only do I gotta work on some lousy *haunting*, I gotta do it for fuckin' free!"

Hans peeked an eye open, judging me silently, then rolled over and faced the window.

Grumbling, I went to get dressed.

My jumpsuit is snug around my wide chest and arms, highlighting my mountainous biceps and protruding pectorals. The material is comparable to a fireman's uniform in terms of strength, but pockets sprouted all over its dense surface, already packed and sagging with various knick-knacks. Metal slots are sewn into the legs, heavy and solid, while a pair of empty sheathes crisscross against the broad back.

I zipped the suit up, stretching out the cutoff sleeves, and went into my armory.

Yes, I said armory. You may have seen those shitty TV shows in which a buncha stupid sweaty dudes bumble around a "haunted" house and piss their panties whenever they hear an especially loud breeze, but that ain't how actual ghost hunting is. You need more than a tripwire and a radio to come against spooks; you need a fucking shotgun.

Hundreds of shells line the walls of my dark armory, coming in a whole range of shapes, sizes, and uses. I yoinked a handful I thought would be especially useful, sliding them one by one into the slots on my legs. In the center of the armory, set nicely into a rack and lit by a contrasting spotlight, was my sawed-off shotgun. I wrenched it from its rack, feeling its impressive weight and studying its intricate design.

The barrel is all solid metal, leading up to a polished wooden stock, the butt of which is encased by a plate of shining silver; every inch of the weapon gleams from the slightest kiss of light. Metal veins swirl up and down the silver like living vines, wrapping around one another and doubling as a sticky grip. A small insignia is stamped between the design: a blocky anvil, encased in swirling metal fire.

I planted a tender kiss to the shotty's barrel, then slipped it into its sheath, sewn into my jumpsuit — one of *two* sheathes; the shotgun was only half the party. Pressing a button hidden underneath the center table, a chunk of the wall spun slowly to reveal the second half...

My greatsword. Five feet of pearly grey radiance, rebounding the spotlight's light like a mirror. I smiled at her...

my Baby.

Hefting her from her rack, I appreciated her astounding weight. For a normal man, she'd be a two-handed weapon — her blade is eight inches across, five feet long, all of pure steel — but not for Graves. Baby spun between my palms, white glinting as she twirled. Metallic clouds swirl up her sides and separate the center of the blade from the razor-sharp edge. The hilt is strong leather, the pommel forged into the vague shape of a five-sided star. My kiss for Baby was much more sensual than for the gun. The shotgun was a weapon, Baby was my partner...

She slid perfectly into her cloth sheath, crossing over the shotgun so both would be within easy reach.

I was ready to fuckin' ride.

And by that, I mean walk. I didn't actually have a car. Or a bike. Or anything rideable in any way. But God saw fit to give me a handsome pair of feet, and *I* saw fit to spend my last check on a nice pair of combat boots. Why not use 'em both?

I thought those happy thoughts for about a third of the five-mile walk to Mallery Jacobs' house. Even with the swirling grey-white clouds high above me, the air in Hartsville was muggy and thick. My breath came roughly, as if through a damp cloth, and my skin was drenched by sweat and atmospheric moisture. I prayed it wouldn't rain.

Hartsville is a tiny town in the heart of good ol' South Carolina, bringing with it all of the humidity, impurity, and general shitiness of its surrounding homeland. The path I walked was bare, just barely showing through the stomped-down yellow grass, crunching beneath my boots. Dirt and dust intermingled with dying crops to my left and right, and that continued for miles at a time, only broken up by the randomly placed barn or farmhouse. Old men and women sat rocking on their porches, staring at me with icy eyes. More often than not, a rifle of some sort lay across their laps. I guess I *did* have a shotgun, but stuff like that is more common than you might think in Hartsville. It's a spooky kind of place, teeming with ancient houses, inexplicable occurrences, and a holy shit-ton of murderous ghosts.

I wasn't sure why, or how, or when, but the tiny town is a hotspot for the undead. That's why I chose to live here — it certainly wasn't the people or the thick, soupy air, that's for fuckin' sure; I wanted to kill ghosts, and lots of 'em. You can barely take a step in the shithole without walking into some years-dead relative, and they're more than often out for blood.

Unluckily for them, so am I.

As I walked, moisture misting on my forehead, I pulled out the manila envelope and read up on the case:

Mallery Jacobs had been haunted for the past few days; some unknown spirits were leaving various spooky messages, such as "die," "bleed," and "love." One of these is clearly unlike the other, and led Mallery to believe her recently dead *husband* was the one behind the haunting. The old bird's selective memory wasn't something to be trusted, so the Union took an interest.

And somehow, someway, Josephi got his greedy, grubby, slimy little hands on it before any of the other hunters...

Oh, wait. Flipping the summary page over, the next paper was entitled *Assigned Hunters.* On the top was written *Graves [LAST NAME]*, which was awfully fuckin' presumptuous of Josephi. And under that, *Gus Beuzzle, of the Spector Detectors...*

The papers crunched in my crushing grip. I gritted my teeth as a house appeared on the horizon; according to the address in the case file, Mallery's. A giant white van sprouted up next to it. On the side was scrawled *Spector Detectors* in

Impact Font.

Whoever this Gus Beuzzle guy was, he just made the 29,000-foot hike up to the tippy-top of the mountain that was my shit list.

Chapter 2

The Hunt

When I pictured Gus Beuzzle, I imagined a stocky, six-foot-tall beefcake with an attitude problem and a death wish. What I found was a chunky 19-year-old in a heavily stitched turtleneck and loose khakis. His brown hair was cut short, a pair of glasses mostly masked his eyes, tucked into a pair of chubby cheeks.

As I strolled up, the hunter was hefting a heavy-looking satellite out of his van, complete with radar dish and beeping red light. When he saw me, his beady eyes bugged out behind his glasses. He dropped the satellite with a *crash*.

"Graves!?" he called, voice cracking.

"Uh... yeah?"

A small smile parted his moist cheeks. "Graves!"

"Yes. Fuckin' Graves."

"Dude! You're, like, a legend! When I saw your name in the case file, I thought it was too good to be true!" He looked like an excited puppy; if he had a tail, it'd be wagging. "What are you doing here!?"

"I'm here to take care of Mallery Jacobs' spook." I stopped in front of him, staring at the chubby teenager with flat eyes. "What are *you* doing here?"

His smile melted away like snow in springtime. "I, uh… I'm here for the same." Beuzzle's eyes fell to his sneakers, one untied. Not as I expected at all.

"Is that so?" I said with false surprise. "There must have been some kind of mix-up, then. See, this is *my* job — and I most certainly will *not* split the fucking pay."

"Uh... um..." Beuzzle mumbled.

"Look at me." He did so, face jiggling gently. "I'm here to take heads from bodies; whether it be a spook's or someone else's is left to be seen. Fuckin' scram."

Beuzzle held the stare. His pupils were shrunken and nervous but there was a glint — a *sparkle* — of rebellion in those eyes. My brow twitched with frustration.

"What are you waiting for?" I asked. "Get the fuck outta here."

"The Union won't allow this," he replied, voice cracking like a patch of rotten ice, giving away his nerves and adolescence. Breaking the stare, Beuzzle reached into his van and whipped out a manila envelope, matching mine. "Says here—" he pointed at a line of dark text "—that *I'm* assigned to this case. I-if forcibly revoked, the Union will... t-take your license."

Moisture leaked from his fingers and soaked into the top of the paper. It trembled within his grasp, and not because of the breeze. The bold text mocked me, like a dozen snapping animals, sharply angled and dangerous to the touch.

"You three already took my last job," I said. "What? One ain't e-fucking-nough for you?" With a *crunch*, I punched the side of the van, leaving a my-hand-sized dent in the metal.

Beuzzle swallowed and stared at where my fist had hit. A dollop of sorrow touched his expression. "I-I'm kinda flying solo, now..."

I laughed. "The other two got tired of you, huh?" He frowned and looked away, letting his hand fall with the paper. Mist grazed his eyelids. Straightening, I considered my options.

I could either boot Beuzzle from the case and risk the Union's wrath, or let the kid play along — or I could kill him, which is an option you types neglect all too often. Sure would save me some trouble...

He sniffled and wiped his nose with the back of his baggy sleeve; the other members of the Specter Detectors must have done him real dirty to beat him up this much.

"Fine," I said. "But we're splitting the pay 70/30."

He flinched. "W-well, I—"

With a predatory silence, I made another dent in the side of the van. He gulped. "S-sounds like a plan!"

I grunted, then turned to observe the Haunt.

Mallery Jacobs' home was ripped straight from a scary story. The walls were made with splintered wood, white paint peeling in long strips to reveal rotting brown, punctured randomly with termite holes. A pair of windows looked out from the top level like a set of lifeless eyes, one left open so its glass doors rattled ~~and banged~~ with the increasing breeze. A red porch sprawled in front of us like a welcoming mouth, the house's front door a window into the black depths of its empty gullet. The clouds seemed to darken as I studied the manor, an ominous shadow casting over this one patch of earth, singling it out as an unholy site.

"Gee," I said, "we sure this place is haunted?"

Beuzzle gave a nervous titter from right next to me. He'd grabbed his hefty satellite, as well as another handful of wires, doohickeys, and even thingamajigs. I'm not great with technology.

Even still, staring at that pile of contraptions told me something: Gus Beuzzle was a medium. I *hated* mediums. They pussyfoot around way too much, trying to fucking *communicate* with the spooks rather than just jumping to the fun part: ripping their asses apart.

My mouth twisted with unveiled disdain. "I think this case is pretty cut and dry. What do you need all *that* for?"

Beuzzle shrugged, smiling down at his satellite like a newborn babe. "You never know. Didn't the case file say something about Ms. Jacobs' *husband* possibly doing the haunting?"

My laugh was booming, even as the porch let out a disconcerting *creak* when I planted my foot on the first step. "Would her husband write 'die' and 'bleed'? Seems kinda fucked up. Pretty sure the file says they were *happily* married, too. How do you explain that, smart guy?"

"By *asking*, of course," he said genuinely, patting one of his devices. "How else?"

I frowned at him, but dropped the argument as we reached the door. When I banged the bronze knocker against the peeling wood, I swore that the entire house was gonna collapse. Instead, the door creaked open, revealing a tiny old woman.

Mallery wore exquisitely white clothing — white hat, white shoes, white blouse and dress — all without a *speck* of the surrounding dust, dirt, or grime on them. Her nose hooked over white-painted lips, which sucked and slurped, presumably on dentures. A wooden cane — carved from white birch — shook underneath her weight. Contrasting it all, her ink-black eyes appraised me disdainfully, ignoring Beuzzle.

"You are the inspector?" she asked in a raspy voice, painted with a classy British accent.

"Graves at your service." I gave a little bow. When I straightened, Mallery had her eyes narrowed.

"I do not approve of weaponry in my household. My old Hickory had no use for them, nor do I."

My brows furrowed with incredulity. "How else am I

supposed to kill the—"

"Graves is here as backup, ma'am!" Beuzzle cut in, struggling underneath his veritable mountain of electronics. "I'm going to confer with Mr. Jacobs and get this all sorted out — don't you worry! Graves won't draw his weapons unless he needs to. Right, Graves?"

I shot him an acidic look. Who the fuck was *this* guy to do my talking for me? I did my jobs how *I* wanted to — and that was always the *best* way. If the kid and this old bird didn't want that... I'd take my services elsewhere. *I don't need that 70*, I thought. *I'll just come back after this kid gets killed, and take care of the spook myself. Simple!*

"Hm. That will be fine, then," Mallery said. "Come along."

Beuzzle stared back apologetically, then shuffled after the old woman and into the haunt. I stood there for a moment, staring into the pitch-blackness that they'd disappeared into.

Fuck it, I thought with stubborn resolve. *Don't wanna walk the ten miles for nothing, do I?*

The inside of Mallery's home was no less creepy than its shell. The wallpaper used to be a pleasant pattern of flowers and leaves, but now it peeled like sunburned skin, bleached and faded and crisped. The halls stretched so far that their ends were dipped in thick darkness, their sides only illuminated by weakly whipping candle flames. Moths fluttered around the alluring fire. Translucent clouds of dust pillowed around my boots with each step, the floorboards growling like beasts underneath my weight.

Wrapping all of these visuals in a soft embrace was the death hum.

You ever walk into an old place and feel a sort of *weight* fall upon you, alongside a dull ambiance? To you people, it would sound like the wind gently blowing through an empty cave at midnight, making the haunt seem ten times larger. To people like *us* — me and the hunters — the hum is like the death rattle of a dying man, stretched and anguished and never-ending. It's a droning moan, just on the *edge* of hearing, but louder the nearer you come to its source.

Mallery led us down one hallway and into a dilapidated kitchen; the cupboards were covered with chipping paint, some hanging by their hinges, water dripped rhythmically from the rusted faucet over the sink — which was filled with dirty dishes, some sprouting bits of moss-green mold. A circular table sat in the center of the kitchen, surrounded by chairs that looked like they'd collapse if I so much as farted on them. Beuzzle threw his supplies onto the table's surface with a relieved sigh; I cringed, waiting for it to collapse, but it remained sturdy.

"So," I started, "about where did you see your 'husband's' first message? And what was it?"

The old woman put a white-painted nail on her wrinkled chin. "It was in the upstairs bathroom... and I believe he wrote 'You die soon,' or something of the like."

I scoffed. "Huh. Some sort of love language between the two of you?"

"I am not quite sure *why* Hickory would write that. And in *blood* no less." She shrugged. "But he was always an odd one. I gathered that even from our short marriage."

"Uh... short?" Beuzzle asked. He sat on one of the wooden chairs, which bent and trembled beneath his impressive girth. "Exactly how long were you and Hickory married, Ms. Jacobs?"

"Three years."

I outright laughed at that. "Late lovers, eh? Good for you."

"Yes, well, Hickory did have his fancies." Mallery donned a look of wistful remembrance. "We only met after his wife had died — awful woman, from the things he told me. I moved into his home... but now it's just mine." She sniffed loudly, then pulled out a white handkerchief and dabbed at her nose. Frowning knowingly, Beuzzle reached over and gripped her hand, comforting the old bird.

"Alright, you two have fun," I said. "I'll be upstairs actually killing the ghost while Beuzzle here tries to play Telephone with it." I snickered and turned to leave.

"K-kill?" Mallery said.

"He only means *help*. Right, Graves?" Beuzzle asked.

"Yeah, sure."

Their voices trailed into whispers as I walked away from the kitchen. At the bottom of the staircase, I looked up to see a dusty red carpet spilling from the top step, which was drenched in dense shadow. It rolled and pooled at my feet, as if some unfortunate soul's neck had been sliced hours-passed, and now his crimson blood flowed like wine down the absorbing wood...

Or maybe it looks like a fucking staircase with a red carpet, I reminded myself. *This is no time to get all poetic.*

I clomped up the steps and towards the endless darkness above. Bleached sunlight leaked through the windows upstairs, streaming from their rooms and out into the hallway that led to each. The beams of light let out their own radiance and illuminated my surroundings. I figured the room at the end of the hall was my destination, so I moved towards it and opened the door.

Inside was a fluffy-looking, well-kept bed with a plush white comforter, white linens, and white pillows. The walls in this room were so clean that they had to be newly painted, in stark contrast to the rest of Mallery's home. Scanning the perimeter, I saw a couple of high-backed chairs, a nightstand on either side of the bed, and a white dresser topped with a shining mirror—

A shadow, strikingly wide-shouldered and of perfectly average height, appeared in front of me, face dark and blank and black. I nearly whipped out my shotgun then and there... but, as I leaped out of masculine fright, the shadow matched my movements perfectly. I gritted my teeth.

Fuckin' mirrors.

Next to the dresser was another door, left ajar. The light seemed to wither and die as it breached that doorway; inside was nothing but starless night. Taking a breath — and trying not to cough from the avalanche of dust that flew down and into my lungs — I scooted into the room.

It was pitch-black — like only-showing-the-cartoon-character's-eyes kind of darkness; I swear I heard little violins plucking as I blinked. Chewing my lip, I pressed a little button on the left breast of my jumpsuit. A crisp beam of brightness streamed out of the flashlight sewn into my shoulder, illuminating... a toilet. So clean that it refracted the beam like water.

I restrained another jump as I saw my own pale face, lit in the bathroom mirror by my flashlight. Jesus, were my cheeks always so gaunt? And the way my brow overshadowed my deep-sunken eyes... smiling, I appreciated my chiseled jaw, ever so slightly cleft. And what was that? A little speckle of red. Had I cut myself shaving or something? I leaned forward to inspect my features...

And my face was caked in dripping blood, splattering and oozing like jellied organs.

"GAH!" I shouted, jumping away. Rapidly pressing the button, my flashlight switched to give a wider but weaker beam. I shined it hastily on the mirror to reveal a maddingly scrawled message.

DIE. RUN. DIE. RUN. DIE. RUN. DIE. RUN. DIE. RUN.

Each word was slashed into the mirror's reflective surface as if it'd left the victim's wrists already shaped. On and on they went, from the top corner to the bottom, *DIE RUN DIE RUNDIERUNDIERUN*. The message left all meaning as I glanced at each rapidly warning word — it was telling me to get out before whatever had wrung out this heap of blood and viscera came for *me*. It was staring at me from deep in the surrounding darkness, waiting to rip my flesh apart and take a vicious, gnawing bite from my soul, all for ignoring its warning.

I smiled and laughed, gripping my shaking belly.

"If you wanted a scrap, all you had to do was fuckin' *say* so, Hickory." Baby whispered as she left her sheathe, radiant inch after radiant inch brightening the small bathroom with holy light. A tiny choir sang as she appeared, empowered as she was by the supernatural's presence. They harmonized and sent goosebumps down my spine. "Come get some, you old freak!"

But, when I rotated back towards the doorway with Baby firmly in my grip, it was not an old man I faced. Far from it.

The spook's face was trapped in a perpetual sneer, bare white teeth left to the open air like a skull's. Long strands of white hair sprouted from her rotting scalp, falling around bone-thin shoulders. Her small, withered breasts were left bare, flesh veined like a bat's wing, nipples blue as ice. Her ribs were pressed sharply against her skin or had messily punctured the flesh. The worst were her eyes: they were like black marbles, jammed into a skull that barely fit, emotionless, unfeeling.

As Baby's light rotated and landed on her form, the spook shrieked — a voice like hundreds of breaking mirrors, a dying choir of crashing glass. Her rotting legs flailing, she flopped in the air and sped away; she didn't expect to be revealed by

Baby's radiance, spooks rarely do.

"Peek-a-boo," I said, stomping towards her writhing form. Bits of translucent slobber leaked between clattering teeth as she snarled. With a siren's wail, she rocketed into the air, then flew at me like a missile.

Baby spinning in my grip, I turned to the side and let the spook fly by, back into the bathroom to be swallowed by the darkness. Her dim luminescence fought off some of the hungry shadows, leaving her an easy target. I leaped towards her with Baby held to my side, ready for a swift, sure slice. The spook slid to the side as lithe as an eel; my Blade sliced through the toilet, *crunching* into and out of the porcelain like paper. Something *thumped* into my side, slamming me into the marble counter to the right and cracking its surface. I shouted with surprise and pain.

More circular objects pummeled against my ribs, forcing me deeper into the counter as if through water. I *rammed* into the mirror. It shattered, flakes of glass falling on me like snow, and their sharp older brothers scratching against my suit and tearing small gouges.

My momentum stopped, but the spook continued its pummeling. After a deep breath, I shouted, flexed my arms and chest, and *destroyed* the counter around me. Baby was sure in my grip, glowing and excited to be back out in the open. The spook reeled, finally easing up its punching, but I quickly followed. Her arm shot forward in an attempt at defense, but Baby whirled and sliced right through her shoulder. The appendage went limp and fell to the ground, puffing into glowing blue-white mist as it landed. Ectoplasm rocketed from the fresh wound in a white torrent, all steaming and misting away like her old flesh. We stared at the mist — my eyes wild and triumphant and distracted, hers sightless and dead and focused.

Shrieking, she hit me in a savage tackle, wrapping her available arm around my shoulders; it somehow coiled around me twice over like a bony, starving snake. We crashed through the wall as if it were made with cardboard, slamming into the hallway beyond and onto the dusty red rug. Teeth clacked as she gnashed at my face. Despite my wriggling, she sank her fangs into my cheek. Before she could tear away a chunk of flesh, I wrenched away with inhuman strength and speed. She stared at me with those black eyes, stunned, then went back to attempt another bite. I met her halfway with my forehead in a savage headbutt.

Her teeth mushed beneath my skull like so many marbles, dislodging and clattering to the wood and rugged floor. The spook screamed and threw me away with insane strength...

I grunted as my shoulders rammed through wall after wall, plaster and bugs and dust coating me. Raucous darkness encased me and, as I fell, I lost all sense of direction or gravity. It was a drunken spiral of ramming pain and swirling black.

I hit something sturdy enough to break my fall, breath rushing out of my lungs in a pained scream.

"*Fuck!*" I yelled. Sharp dust flew down my throat when I gasped, making me cough out decades' worth of debris.

"What on Earth?" someone asked, voice raspy.

"Graves!? What's going on!?" Beuzzle said with his nasally tone.

Groaning, I sat up and blinked the dust out of my eyes. I'd landed on Mallery's kitchen table, narrowly missing the medium's equipment. Bits of sheetrock and wallpaper and wood sprinkled from the hole in the ceiling that someone had just made. I stared at it groggily, then looked at Mallery, whose face was stretched in horror.

"Sturdy fuckin' table, huh?"

Beuzzle's hands were clenched nervously to a metal box, a speaker bulging from its center. His fingers glowed a dull blue, the color leaking and encasing the spirit box in his fists. Suddenly, words spilled from Beuzzle like water from a spigot. "Graves! I got in touch with Hickory Jacobs' spector! He stuck around to *warn* Mallery about something — someone, maybe, I don't know; we were still talking with him when... Well, anyway, I've got somc theories and—"

"Could it possibly be his ex-wife?" I croaked. Looking towards Mallery, I asked, "She didn't happen to die in this house, did she?" She nodded shakily.

Beuzzle flinched, then looked at the ceiling thoughtfully. "Huh... I hadn't thought of that."

An echoing shriek spilled from the dark hole as if it were an opened maw. Two balls of light stared down at me, hungry and inhuman, but the rest of the spook was masked by shadow.

"Oh, shit."

"What is *that*!?" Beuzzle said. He dropped his device with a *crash*, the white-blue spectral energy fading from his fingertips like light from a dying bulb. "Is that her, Graves!? Oh, Jesus!"

"Dumbass," I growled, rolling off the table with Baby still glowing in my clenched fist. "Get the old bird to safety. *NOW!*"

The moment that Beuzzle went to obey my command, Hickory's ex-wife exploded from the hole, rushing at Mallery with her single claw outstretched. The old woman screamed and stumbled away, staring at the spook's biting teeth and wicked eyes. If the ghost moved even a few more inches, Mallery would've been toast.

Luckily, I'm me.

With precision and grace, I leaped from the table and into

the air, twisting my body in mid-flight so Baby's radiant tip pointed at the spook's fleeing back. Snarling, I drove the Blade through her torso; I was rewarded with a sudden and shrill scream. The spook and I went crashing to the floor, my greatsword puncturing her ghostly flesh and stabbing into the old wood with a *thud.* Ectoplasm sprayed everywhere, leaking from this new wound and her gnashing mouth alike. With a victorious grunt, I swiped Baby to the right; she ate through spectral organs and flesh and bone like nothing, finally exploding from her ribs in a spray of glowing viscera.

Now whimpering pathetically, the half-bisected spook rolled onto its back and fixed me with those dark pupils. I smiled wolfishly back.

Then took her head from her shoulders with a single jab, Baby puncturing and prying off her neck like a cork. White blood shot outwards like champagne, dousing Mallery. Breathing heavily, I sat in one of the chairs and watched as each bit of spectral flesh and ectoplasm misted away, evaporating like water in a pot. Hickory's ex was on her way to the Other Side — the Spectral Plain, most like.

"Yeah, bitch," I panted. "Gotcha."

"W-what... what have you done?" Mallery asked.

"What do you mean? I got rid of your spook — easy as pie." I rubbed at my dully aching ribs, where Hickory's ex had continuously socked me. "You don't sound very grateful."

"*Grateful?* Look at my home — Hickory and my home! This was what was left of my husband, the love of my life. And look what you've done!" She gestured a bone-thin, wavering arm at the hole in the ceiling.

"Hey," I said, shrugging, "them's the ropes of hunting. Some property damage is worth your life, am I right?"

"Graves," Beuzzle whispered. "If you could have *waited...*

waited for me to speak with Hickory and get to the bottom of things, we could have dealt with his ex-wife more... subtly." His face was frightened, yet confident. He had to work up a lot to stand up to me.

The kid should've known better.

"Oh what-the-fuck-ever. Way I see it, *I* did the work, while you sat on your ass and had a nice chat." Beuzzle frowned at me, but said nothing. Mallery wheezed a dry sob into her palm, slowly observing the ruined kitchen. I growled and pointed in the medium's chubby face. "Send me my money, then deal with the rest. I'll be waiting."

Beuzzle made a piping, whining noise, stopping me as I stomped out of the room. "G-Graves... I c-can't pay you."

Oh, now he'd fucking done it. I turned on my heel and grazed him with eyes of fury. "What."

"J-Josephi... he got the contract for me. *He*'s the one paying. Y-you'll have to speak with him in his office—"

He cut off as I punched a gaping hole in the wall; a beam of sudden sunlight streamed through, painting my flat features. We stared at each other — Beuzzle frozen with terror — then I turned and left without another word, steps measured and thudding.

Chapter 3

Deluxe Package

Josephi's office was in downtown Hartsville, so I had a fat fuckin' walk ahead of me; my shack is in the center of the forest, which grows perfectly between the town and the farmland where Mallery lives. This time, though, I had seething determination fueling each of my trudging steps.

Josephi Hostephony had already fucked me over once, now this? Cutting my pay to ribbons — pay I already *owed* him? He was playing a game, and I wouldn't be one of his pawns. Clearly, he'd wanted to take advantage of poor Beuzzle, too, but I'd showed him what was fucking what!

Before I knew it, after a few hours of steady walking, I was at the edge of downtown. The actual *city* part of Hartsville looks like someone dumped out a bucket of children's blocks. Each building is a different color, size, and shape; some are squat and a pale yellow, others cubic with a cherry-red roof.

Regardless, I'd recommend flipping a coin before entering one unannounced, because there's a fifty-fifty chance that it'll be a crack den, and the other fifty percent is a shitty food joint, a smoke shop, or a grimy bar stuffed with unruly characters. Hartsville isn't *just* a hotspot for the supernatural; it attracts criminals and homeless and drug addicts like mice to good gouda. A few pieces of the tiny town are sectioned off and deemed *suburbia*, but more often than not, all you'll find is one shithole after another.

In contrast, though, was Josephi Hostephony's office. It sat between a pair of dilapidated houses, their windows shattered and bricks chipped; the building was a single clean spot on the filthy dish that was that street. Plush green bushes sprouted in front of its red-bricked walls, dotted with colorful flowers and trimmed to smooth-edged perfection. It wasn't a tall or large building, but it didn't need to be; Josephi took his clients one at a time, demanding that they make appointments over the phone weeks in advance. That was part of his money-making strategy: make your client squirm until they're ripe as an orange, then juice them for all they're worth.

A sign hanging over the door's little window read *Josephi Hostephony: Officially Licenced Medium and Union Contractor.*

I scoffed. *Union Contractor* isn't even a real fucking position. What he *meant* to write was *Stupid Fucking Rip-Off Artist.*

As for Josephi being a medium: I've got more power from the Other Side in my dickhead than he has in his whole body. He's a fucking fraud, just like the guys you see on TV, squealing at the slightest shadow.

The only *medium* he'd ever be was medium *rare* under the fire that was my fury.

The doorknob was stiff against the twist of my wrist, but I snarled and kept twisting until it broke clean off. With a touch of a toe, the door swung inwards easily.

The rat's office was just as I remembered: cream plaster for the walls, red velvet for the furniture, red trimmed with gold for the carpet. It smelled like fresh cookies and springtime. Hostephony furnished like he lived: pompous, perfumed, phony, and in your fucking face. To my right was a polished wooden desk, manned by the woman who'd visited me earlier. Her lovely blue eyes were wide with surprise.

"Afternoon, ma'am." My teeth flashed. "Did you miss me?"

"Mr. Graves—"

"It's just Graves," I corrected, still smiling like a hungry dog.

"Just Graves, then. Mr. Hostephony has no open appointments today."

"Oh?" I looked behind me, then to either direction. "You're talking to me? Because I don't remember asking." I gently placed my palms on the desk. "Now, you can beep Josephi and let him know I'm coming, or I can make it a pleasant little surprise."

Her burgundy-painted lips pursed and twisted, her eyes ice-cold and filled with annoyance. I love it when a woman stares at me that way — shows me that they'd be a challenge. I smiled at her knowingly, then straightened and moved towards Josephi's office. Rather than test my strength against the door's knob, I pulled it off immediately and saved myself a few seconds.

A lovely pair of women sat inside Josephi's office, well-toned legs slipping out of their pencil skirts, revealing inches and inches of smooth brown skin. Their hair was pluming and bushy, mostly black but intermingled with strands of hazel. Two pairs of arms crossed impatiently over two pairs of generously sized bosoms. Matching pearl necklaces hung around their necks, each sphere of white shining like a miniature star. The twins glared at me with frustrated chocolate eyes.

"Um, we're in a meeting right now," one of them said.

"I see that," I said.

Josephi was at his desk in front of them. He's a white guy with a medium build, medium height, and fatherly face. He has black hair — grey on the sides — that constantly looks wet. Every stitch of his suit was worth more than my shoes, plus the gold watch wrapped around his pale wrist, the gold crucifix hanging from his neck, and the seven rings studding some of his fingers, each golder than my piss at midnight. He had his hands by his head, two fingers touching either temple. His eyes were shut and he was nearly motionless; I could barely even see him breathing.

"Lemme guess, the Deluxe Package?" I snickered. "What's that? One question answered?"

The other twin jumped, surprised.

"Don't feel too bad. You're not the first suckers he's caught with that one. And you definitely won't be the last."

"Suckers?" one demanded, belligerent. "Mr. Hostephony has proven to be quite accurate on *Answers From the Other Side.*"

Answers From the Other Side was Josephi's side hustle, a show in which he fooled poor dopes into thinking he was actually conferring with their dead relatives.

I scratched at my chin like a detective piecing together a problem. "Let's see here… Two middle-aged women, both seemingly well-endowed — in the wallet, I mean — and most likely very attached to their wealth, both seeing a medium to have a very important question answered. Dead parent, I figure?" One twin glared daggers through my heart, while the other one nodded pensively.

"Rich daddy?"

They both gave no reaction this time.

"Uh-huh. Watch this." I closed my eyes and put my fingers to my temples, mimicking the false medium in front of us.

"Josephi — I mean your dad, apologies — is about to say…" I made ghostly humming noises, building the tension, then leaned down and whispered, "... that you two will have to split the fortune."

They both gave one another the glariest of glares, then set high beams on Josephi. While they waited anxiously for him to "wake up," I grabbed a few pencils from his desk and flung them at him. The twins gasped as the pencils *whacked* the conman on the side of the head, but he didn't flinch.

If there's one thing Josephi is good at, it's acting.

After a few more minutes, Josephi opened his eyes with a sharp inhale. He grinned fatherly at the twins, then faked surprise when he looked at me. I rolled my eyes and moved two fingers in a circle, giving him the "speed it up" gesture.

Josephi cleared his throat and said, "Ladies, your father gives his greetings." His voice was smoother than silk, like a saxophone by moonlight. "He says that he is quite happy and thinks of you regularly. He wants to know how your mother is…?" Neither of them jumped to answer the question, instead squinting their eyes at him skeptically. I stifled a laugh.

Josephi took it all in stride. He smiled at them — he even flashed his teeth towards me, the bastard — then said, "I see. Well, your father figured that the object of inheritance would come up, and was worried that the fortune would come between you. He said, and I quote, 'You're two peas in a pod. S'always been that way; always will be if I've got anything to say about it.'" He touched his accent with a dollop of Southern. "You've been sharing everything since you were girls — my love, most of all. I just want what's best for you. Both of you.'"

Drum roll, please, I thought.

"'S'why,'" Josephi continued, "'I think you, my lovely

girls, should split the fortune evenly. For the love of mine you share and the bond that can't be broken between you, take my money and build something *together*.'"

Ha!" I said. "You're too easy, Hostephony!" I spun out of the chair and pulled open the door for the twins, gesturing out with a sweeping wave. "After you, ladies. Don't say I didn't warn you..."

But they weren't bustling out in anger. Not even in a huff. They weren't bustling out at *all*, in fact.

The bimbos were streaming tears and hugging each other, for Christ's sake! Blubbering like babies!

Sometimes I forgot just how good a conman Josephi really was; the guy was *born* to cheat, *bred* to steal, a ball of conniving filth rolling around in human form. Well, I wouldn't be another one of his fuckin' suckers. Not this time.

The buxom twins thanked Josephi profusely, shaking his hand and scribbling down something on a piece of paper. They left without another word for me, still crying and apologizing to one another. I stared in disbelief.

Josephi's chair squeaked as he sat back down and tucked the slip of paper into one pocket.

"Don't tell me, you got one of their numbers." His smile was whiter than the twins' pearls. "Fucking *both*?"

The conman shrugged with a subtle cockiness, then steepled his fingers and stared at me with eyes as black as frostbitten hands.

"What can I do for you, Graves? If you couldn't tell, I was in the middle of a meeting."

"Don't you try to pull that shit with me, asswipe," I said, pointing my finger warningly at him. "You know *exactly* why I'm fuckin' here."

Josephi shook his head and tsked three times. "Graves, Graves, Graves. Always with the language. Maybe you could spell out what you mean in more clear terms? I'd love to help you with any problem that may be ailing you."

"Let's not beat around the bush, Hostephony, you little piece of *slime*. I owe you money — yeah, you swindled me out of it, but that's how it works up here. I will pay you back for getting me that job, as much of a con as it was. But..." I leaned forward and let my upper lip curl in bestial rage, "if you try to manipulate me again, I'll pay you back with a dent in your fucking skull."

Horror flashed over his black eyes, but he cleared his throat and dispelled it. "Manipulate...? What are you talking about, Graves?"

"Gus Beuzzle, dipshit. You assigned him Mallery's case, *trying* to half my pay, *knowing* that I couldn't do shit to him with the Union watching over my shoulders. I know how you operate — even if I don't know *why*, I know *when*. Let me repeat: If I get so much as a fuckin' *whiff* of your brand of fuckery, I'll slaughter you like the greedy, snuffling pig that you *are*. Is that clear?" I let an inhuman rage wash over my features, fists and head trembling in barely-restrained anger.

The Union protects its members — even this stupid piece of shit. If I killed him, or even beat his ass, the Union would be close behind to not only revoke my license, but to potentially *arrest* me, or even worse.

But sometimes people can be a little *unpredictable*, right? Sometimes that flare of sudden fury is all it takes for someone to lose all control and lose their fuckin' mind. As I glared at Josephi, I could see the glue that held his facade together melting like wax. He believed, he knew that I'd keep my promise if he kept pushing me. What did one measly debt mean to a dead guy?

Yet he clung on. "G-Graves. You cannot mean that. We're *business* partners—"

Wordlessly, I reeled back and slapped him across the cheek — not at my full strength, as that was liable to break some bones but hard enough to make Josephi stagger with the blow and cry out like a little girl.

"Okay, okay, Graves!" he whimpered. "I'm juss tryin' to make an honest livin' here, honest! No need to get rowdy, yee-ah?" His inner Brooklynite was showing, the face he didn't show his Southern crowd on *Answers From the Other Side*. Black strands of smoothly slicked hair were now loose and hanging around his pale skin, surrounding eyes now swimming in fear.

"Fucker, the only honest bone in your body is the one in your shriveled *cock*." I straightened, glaring at the pathetically shaking conman. "Now, let me work. You'll get your damn money when *I* say so, no sooner. Remember this—" I put my hand up, the one I'd used to slap him "—and think about what it could do if I didn't hold myself back."

Josephi rubbed his reddening cheek, saying nothing more. I stared at him flatly, then turned to make my leave.

But of course, *of course*, the little fucker had something else to say.

"Graves! Hold on there! I got somethin' that might help you!"

"Anything *you're* selling, Hostephony, I ain't fucking buying. Go back to the puddle of piss you crawled out of."

"Graves! I'll pay three times the Union price!" he yelled after me. I gritted my teeth, but remained steadfast.

"Fuck off," I yelled back. The secretary looked at her hands politely.

"You might tink twice if you saw who the client was!" he pleaded. "She's quite the lookah ya know." I stopped. "Famous... and stinkin' filthy rich!"

My clenched fists shook by my side. No way was I buying

this. I was not gonna fucking fall for another one of Josephi's stupid tricks...

Not for free, anyhow.

I stomped back into his office. "*Four* times the Union price, half up front and the rest towards our debt. Then we're fucking square, Josephi. No ifs, asses, or titties. Get me?"

"You bet! You gotta deal!" He stuck his hand out for shaking.

"Just give me the case file," I growled.

Smiling stupidly, the conman reached into a safe behind his desk and drew out a thick folder, teeming with papers.

"If I may make a recommendation for youse, Graves, I would suggest working with a medium on this one. Maybe Gus Beu—"

"You may fucking not. I work alone — you'd best remember that." I snatched the folder from his hands, dully aware that I had probably just made a huge mistake.

My mind knew it, my heart knew it.

But my dick didn't.

And in the end, once I got a look of the headshot of my newest client, that guy was calling the shots.

Chapter 4

History

Holy bouncing boobies, Batman! I thought, still ogling at Jennifer Nee's picture.

The Jennifer Nee! I hadn't lived on... *in* Hartsville long, but I still knew who she was.

Jennifer Nee is a pop idol, responsible for songs such as *Kiss Me and Love Me*, *A Night in Your Dreams*, and *Temptation so Sweet*, each a soliloquy of sexual pride and feminine power. Her sweet voice makes my heart race and hips gesticulate like nothing else... not to mention her big fat titties. *Can't* forget those!

I was still drooling over her headshot when I got back to my forest shack, feet aching and pants maybe just a little tighter than normal. Hans thanked me with a leg rub when I filled his bowl, then curled up next to me on the couch and purred, immediately asleep. Finally tearing my eyes away from Jenny's cleavage, I flipped the page and read up on her case.

Apparently, Ms. Nee had bought one of the largest — actually, no, *the* largest — mansion in Hartsville. Shortly after moving in, the popstar began hearing, quote, "spooky moaning" coming from underneath her house. The police were called but, after endless searching and digging, they came up with nothing. The moaning was chalked up as growing pains for a decades-old house, then the officers packed up and left — your hard-earned tax dollars at work, folks. Nee called the Union, Josephi caught a whiff and got his hands on the case, now here I was reading about it. Seemed pretty cut-and-dry: Get under the house, either kill a spook or do some plumbing, flexing whatever body parts I could, then maybe get a little something extra from Jenny, who knows...?

A man can dream.

As listed on the next page, the mansion had been vacated for over forty years, after its previous owner, Erick Horst, was arrested for treason. Yes, treason; the guy was a fucking' *Nazi*. He was an intel agent for the US during the second World War, then going by the name Eric Johnson (possibly the most American name ever). Erick was *supposed* to be getting intel about the Reich — which, technically, he did; the Germans fed him whatever info they didn't mind sharing, along with a few sacks of cash, and all Erick had to do was trade precious U.S. secrets. He was caught, but whatever happened afterwards is fuzzy. Some think that our military brained him, others think that they used him as a double agent, and a select few think Erick is still out there, haunting our bases.

Nazis and conspiracies, right next to peaches and cream.

An annoying little gnat buzzed inside my head, a stinging ball of inconvenient logic. I've seen movies, I've read some comic books, and I have a modest collection of paperbacks; I know how shit like this goes. Spooky moaning, Nazi's abandoned mansion — like, come on. But life isn't a *movie*, it's fucking *life*. If stories came true, I'd have a harem of Disney princesses by now. Get real.

Still, that gnat bit at my frontal lobes, insisting that something stunk in Jennifer's mansion.

It also said, "Hey, stupid. Don't forget who gave you this

case. Keep your big dumb eyes open." I decided to listen to my little bug friend.

Smiling to myself, I looked at Hans; he stared back at me with one eye, judging me for my dormant schizophrenia.

"What am I supposed to do? Talk to *you*? Don't be crazy." Hans sniffed and went back to sleep.

Sleep. What a *marvelous* idea.

I gave Baby a nicc polishing — and gave her a goodnight kiss — then put her back on her rack. I did the same with my shotty, jamming a little brush in and out of its barrel and scraping off any gunk, despite not having fired it a single time that day; can't be too careful with that kind of shit. After staring at the pair longingly for a few moments, I shut off the light and locked up my armory.

My bedroom was sparse. A bed — and by that, I mean a hard rectangular object that I'd scrounged out of the dump — was flush with one wall. I had a spare jumpsuit hanging in a closet opposite, which was nice since Hickory's ex-wife had done a number on the one I was wearing. And that was about it... other than some of Hans' little "gifts." Thanks for that, cat.

Air rushed out of me as I flopped onto my bed, ambiguous metal objects scraping inside of it. Hans, hearing me go to bed, ran into my room and jumped onto my back. After circling a few times, he found a comfortable place on my shoulders and flopped down. His purring lulled me slowly to sleep.

Something bright tenderly pressed onto the insides of my eyelids. At first, I thought it was the sun, rising above the hills surrounding Hartsville like the rim of a bowl. But, as my brain rebooted after my deep sleep and I thought for a moment, I realized that the light was decidedly pinker than anything our natural sun could make.

My retinas shrunk painfully when I cracked my lids open. A pink aura floated in my bedroom, slowly dimming around its edges. In its center sprouted a pretty little face with pale skin and a feminine curve. Plush lips underneath an upturned nose caught my attention, and when she opened her eyes, they were a creamy black.

"Graves," the aura intoned, pillowy lips hardly moving. Her voice was a waterfall of song. I sat up, rubbing the sleep from my eyes, and stared into the heavenly light. Her eyes stared back, emotionless.

"The fuck do you want, Agatha," I asked.

Her face didn't change, but the light surrounding it dimmed enough to reveal the slight outline of her curvaceous body. "Only to see you punished for your crimes, as any denizen of the Other Side would."

I'd been waiting for this. "'Punished for my crimes,'" I quoted. "Yeah, I'm sure there are a *lot* of 'denizens' coming for me. But you're not just a *denizen*, are you?"

Agatha's lips spread in a cute smile. "No. Nonetheless, you have committed unimaginable atrocities, and I mean to see you repent."

I scoffed. "As if you could get away with that."

Agatha ignored me. "You are to bring me a host, Graves; someone whose form I can inhabit and use to root myself in the physical realm."

"Uh... No? Why the hell would I do that?"

"Because, if you don't—"

"You'll what? Kill me?" I barked a laugh.

The white radiance blinked off like a lightbulb, fully revealing her plump hips and perky chest. I flinched back and let my eyes crawl up each curve... until I reached her face, once so pretty and comely. Now, the skin had sloughed off like ground beef, splatting on my concrete floor and freeing skeletal, fanged teeth and jade-like purple bones. Her eyes went wide — or maybe that was just because the flesh around them had dripped away — and their tiny green pupils landed on me with focused fury. Twin fangs clattered as she spoke. "Yes. I will kill you." Her voice was like metal in a meat grinder.

I cleared my throat. "Um... you got the OK from the Big Guy, then?"

Agatha's purple skull nodded up and down, eyes never detaching from mine. I swallowed. That was not fuckin' good.

Agatha is a deity from the Other Side — the Afterlife, meaning. Heaven and Hell, Hades and Mount Olympus, Valhalla and so on. They're all the same place, rolled into a neat little ball we dub the Other Side, for simplicity's sake. Not only that, but the place is home to all sorts of beasts and monsters and downright bothersome critters, most straight of storybooks. It's an endless expanse of horror and death and blood, much larger than the mortal realm... and I have a history with the place. A history now coming back in the form of Agatha, here to rip me apart for a crime those in the Other Side *think* I committed.

I had assurances that no one from the Other Side — whether it be the Bowels or the Gates or what have you — could do me any harm. It looked like that assurance now came with a price.

"A host?" I asked, rubbing my chin. "That's not so bad. I can pluck any idiot off the street."

At my words, Agatha's violet teeth somehow curled upwards in a malicious grin. "You wish it could be so simple, Graves. But the Reaper has decided to make a test of this."

"Of course," I sighed. "You gods and your stupid fucking games. I'll never escape them, will I?"

She clucked her teeth. "Doubtful."

"What is it this time? A pure-minded virgin? Three hundred men Voltroned into one giant man? What kind of host is so crucial?"

"Something that, if you are innocent of your accused crimes, should come easily to you, Graves." Like paint being splattered on a blank canvas, skin reformed on Agatha's skull. Hair sprouted from her bare purple scalp, flowing locks black as midnight, smooth as silk. A white gown spun around her, sleeves draping over her dainty hands, bust and waist just a *little* too tight, highlighting every inch of her delectable curves.

Never have I been so put off by a smoking hot chick.

She reached me and leaned forward, putting her doll-like face in front of mine. "You must claim a host with an even more *wicked* heart than yours. Someone responsible for acts more vile than any you have done."

"Oh... is that all?" I laughed in her face. "Easy! Because I'm innocent, dumb-dumb."

"Keep telling yourself that," she snarled. "As if that wipes your slate clean! Truly, I cannot imagine a more terrible *mortal* than you!" Agatha emphasized the word *mortal*. These types loved to rub that in — my ability to die, I mean.

"Why the fuck do you even care so much? And don't try to pull the 'just retribution' act. You and I both know you're the least *just* bitch this side of Hell."

I expected her to delve into uncontrollable rage at the insult, but she simply smiled. "It is your Blade, Bastard. The Blade of Balance... *Chronalius*. Through your conquest, you have earned her obedience, but now it is *my* turn."

I frowned. Yeah, that made sense.

Baby — or Chronalius, as these types like to call her — has a mind of her own. She can choose her wielder, it just so happens that she likes the strongest person in the room, meaning that Baby can only be in the hands of her previous owner's killer...

But I was the exception; she'd been *given* to me by someone close. The moment Baby had fallen into my mitts, I knew that she'd bring with her all sorts of ravenous demons and ghosts and gods or what have you, just *aching* for a chance to rip her away from me. They'd never *succeed,* obviously, but it was still gonna be a bitch to get them off my ass.

Luckily, Baby is also a sick ass greatsword. I'd say that balanced things out.

Agatha was the first of the many buzzing gnats I'd have to swat out of my life, and said swatting would be annoying. Even if I was innocent of the crime they were accusing me of, I still... Well, I've done some bad shit, I'll say that. It wasn't gonna be easy to find someone I truthfully believed more *wicked-hearted* than I was, but what the fuck else was I gonna do?

Agatha seemed to be waiting for the rise she was baiting out of me, but instead, I gave her a charming grin. "You're a princess of Hell, a demoness of some small renown, yet you still don't *get* it, Agatha."

"What knowledge could you, a lowly, short-lived mortal, have over *me*?" She let out an airy scoff. "If the Reaper allowed it, I could easily squish you beneath the weight of my endless mind — reveal such secrets that your worthless brain would leak from your ears in gooey pink paste!"

I put a finger to my chin in mock thought. "Hm. Perhaps, perhaps. But, dear Agatha, you're forgetting something." I leaned forward, bringing my face inches from hers, which was stricken with a subtle confusion, her thin brows furrowed and plush lips petulant. "I have the Blade of Balance, and you don't. So, before you go threatening, remember who the *real* threat is and count yourself lucky that I haven't killed you already."

Finally, I earned the reaction I'd wanted. Her features curdled like week-old cottage cheese. Agatha reeled back into a threatening stance, glaring down at me with pitch-black eyes. "You have two days, 48 hours, to deliver a host with—"

"A more wicked heart than mine. I get it."

"If you *don't*," she snarled, "I will ki—"

"You'll *try* to kill me. And I'll be fucking ready. See you in a few days, babe."

"Midnight," was all she said. Then, with a final glare and a blinding flash of white light, Agatha vanished. I imagined her stomping around in her palace, down in the fiery pits of the Bowels, throwing an even *more fiery* tantrum. She'd *really* wanted to kill me. Robbing her of that felt nice...

For now. I talk a big talk, I know, and I can more than often walk that talk up with a big ass walk, but Agatha wasn't a pushover. She may not have been a full god, but I wasn't even a *demi*-god. It'd be a tough scrap, and not one I wanted to risk. I enjoy a good brawl as much as the next hunter, but I liked living too.

Plus, Agatha with the Blade of Balance... just thinking of that made my stomach do a backflip. I don't know *what* the fuck the Reaper was thinking when he made that deal with her. She put on a good face, but she was butt-fuck insane. If she had Chronalius, the world would be anything *but* balanced.

I blinked and saw a hellscape: Buildings like mountains crumbling beneath Agatha's might, soul after soul falling before her, unsatisfied yet dying all the same, the sky and the streets and the oceans dripping red with blood and viscera. She would kill wantonly, simply for the fun of it. And I don't think she would stop even there. There's only one place to go once you've killed everyone, and that's back down to Hell, with the Blade of Balance secured in her grip...

Baby was entrusted with me so I could *prevent* shit like that, otherwise I would've been pretty apathetic about the whole ordeal. It was my rcsponsibility to keep her out of Agatha's hands, and away from any other malicious asshole from the Other Side. My life was just a bonus.

Tomorrow, I'd go wrap up Jennifer Nee's case, settle up with Josephi, then grab a host for Agatha ASAP. I'd even buy a little bow to put on the poor schmuck's head.

Thinking of that and smiling, I drifted back to sleep with Hans rumbling on my belly.

I dreamed of reaping souls and ink-black eyes…

Chapter 5

Up and Down

Actual sunlight woke me hours later. Hans was a black ball of heat on my chest, warding off a bit of the autumn morning's chill. Still, I scratched him on the head and moved him off. This wasn't a day for sleeping in, it was a day for kicking ass and killing some shit. Usually, those weren't mutually exclusive, but Agatha's appearance had brought a whole load of unfortunate realities.

Knowing I no longer had the Reaper's protection... that weren't no good. It made me feel naked. I realized that having Baby and my shotty hot against my back would help my mood a little, so I stood and went to get ready.

After dressing in my non-torn jumpsuit and slipping both Baby and my shotgun in their perfectly-sized sheathes, I went to work selecting the day's supply of ammunition. It's a more complex task than you'd think, as I've got, like, a *billion* types of shells. There's incendiary rounds shaped like jagged red comets; batteries molded into bullets that'll fry a man's brain in seconds; powerful green acid in thin, shell-shaped gelatin; sticky bombs; tranquilizing darts; heat-seeking shells; you fuckin' name it, big boy.

I've got a supplier who keeps me locked and loaded at pretty much all times. He charges in blood, as many gods do, but every drop's worth it for those sweet, sweet shells.

I snatched the ones I thought most appropriate — meaning

the shells that covered the most bases, since I really had no clue what I was getting myself into — then did myself a favor and called a taxi. Even if I cringed at the price, I'd had enough fucking walking for one adventure.

"You must be outta your mind living here!" the taxi driver said as I walked out of my shack. "It's in the middle o' nowhere!"

"Uh, does it look like I *built* the place, dude? Just drive. And don't even *think* of asking for an extra tip just because my home isn't on your GPS."

The cabby grumbled as I ducked into the taxi, but grew oddly silent as he noticed the stock of my shotgun and the hilt of my greatsword poking out from behind my shoulders. Weird.

His face grew incredulous when I gave him the address, then slowly melted into downright disbelief as we rolled towards a certain part of town. The further we drove, the nicer the houses got; they went from ramshackle crack dens made with cheap brick, to nice suburban homes, freshly-painted and furnished. Their lawns were cleanly cut, not a weed out of place, and each car was nicer than the one before it. A few people raised their hands and waved at us amicably, some playing catch with their kids, or washing their sportscar, or trimming their hedges — you know, rich people stuff.

Yeah, maybe my floor was concrete and my mattress was ancient and my walls were sheets of metal... but did they have an armory? Don't think so.

After we'd driven about a mile through Hartsville's suburb, we reached a metal gate with a metal box to its right. The letters *E J* were set into the gate's center — Eric Johnson, I assumed; this place really had been untouched since his passing. A red-bricked road started after the gate and travelled upwards to a black spot, way in the distance. It was a veritable mountain, dotted with pine trees and flat plains of grass, turned damp and glistening by the night's dew. The entire plot of land made up at least *a fifth* of Hartsville alone.

The cabby peeked back at me and nodded towards the closed gate. "This the end of the road, or...?"

I reached into my jumpsuit and pulled out Nee's case file. Inside, I found a photo-copied notebook page with the number *1933* written on it. The cabby leaned out towards the metal box and punched in the number, and sure enough, the gates creaked open, splitting the *E* and *J* apart.

Racking my brain, I remembered that 1933 was the year a certain ambitious German politician had come into power. Very fucking subtle, Horst.

The red-bricked road winded back and forth, sometimes sandwiched between two lines of unkempt hedges, other times by wilting flower beds. Either way, the closer we came to the hill's top, the more unruly the plant life became; the pine trees grew thicker, becoming a disorderly forest before long. Rolling down the window, I took a few whiffs of the air. It was earthy and sweet, nothing like a manor's lawn would be, more like uninhabited nature.

Then came the mansion.

It slowly rolled over the hill's crest as we traversed the cracked bricks, dark and foreboding and solid. Now, I saw it was more a castle than a manor. The walls were made with dark-grey brick, so uncared for that it looked more like ancient stone. They ran flat and long, longer than any building I'd ever seen, and led to a towering turret on either side. The turrets were crowned with black cones, like stone wizard caps reaching towards the sky. What set the manor apart from medieval architecture was the myriad of glass windows set into its side, like dozens of spider's eyes, weighing its prey as it approached. Through those eyes, I saw only darkness.

The road widened into a sort of cul-de-sac in front of the mansion, spilling into an asymmetrical puddle of red. It was cracked and teeming with relentless weeds, as was the rim of the manor.

Even from here, the death hum was audible, like the sorrowful moaning of a dying animal. I shivered and stared at the mansion's heavy doors.

"How long you gonna wait, pal?" the cabby asked, eyes glued to the mansion's exterior.

I paid the man and climbed out. He sped away with disconcerting haste, engine revving and tires screeching. Then I was alone. The mansion's shadow encased me, blotting out the early morning sun. The droning hum was an endless, ominous reminder of my mission.

The wooden door rang hollowly as I rapped my knuckles against it. There weren't any cars parked around, so I wasn't even sure that anyone actually *did* live here. With a grimace, I realized this could easily be a trap laid by Josephi... or even Agatha. I'm not sure what either of them could have left here for me, but the reality was there all the same.

Maybe a big cartoon safe would fall on me from above, crushing me and making my teeth play like piano keys. Maybe I watch too much TV.

Finally, the door sort of *popped* open an inch, then swung all the way inwards.

And I almost fell on my knees in prayer to the sight before me.

Jennifer Nee was like a beam of God's sunlight — a brilliant gift to the realm of mortals that only the good Lord above would be so generous to present us with. Her hair fell in lazy muddy-blonde puffs, mind-numbingly sexy even when unkempt and bed-roused. Every inch of her skin was unblemished and pale as milk, especially that of her legs, which were bare and revealed underneath her loose shirt. Clearly a man's, the shirt draped over her buoyant, braless chest like a teasing curtain thinly outlining the shape of what lay behind. Her face was young and mature at once, with smart blue eyes and a cute, thin mouth. Jennifer raised a golden eyebrow at me, thin lips curving upwards in an amicable smile.

I pulled my jaw off the ground and resisted the urge to howl towards the sky in an expression of uncontrollable lust. "Hello, Ms. Nee." I gave her my best smile, keeping my posture straight and chest firm. "I'm Graves. Josephi told you I was coming."

"That's right!" Jennifer said. Her voice was rich milk mixed with a dollop of the sweetest honey. "You're here about the moaning. I thought no one would *ever* come after the police gave up. How is a girl supposed to get her sleep with all that noise?" she asked genuinely.

"You could always moan back," I blurted. My cock had taken full control.

Jennifer giggled, things jiggled, my mind fuzzed. "You're funny." She smiled — something to kill over — then reached forward and gripped my bare bicep. Her smooth touch sent an electric shiver up and down my body. I felt drool pooling behind my lips as her eyes met mine, crinkling at the sides with her bright grin.

Get your head in the game, Graves, I thought. *The* right *fuckin' head.*

I cleared my throat and said, "Can I come in?"

The mansion's insides were more modern than its exterior. The floor was black marble, veined with angular bits of white, like lightning cracking in a starless sky. The walls were still dark brick, but they were cleaner and more symmetrical on this side. They were totally bare, though, as all of Horst's paintings and decorations had fled with him. We were in the foyer, which was as stretched as an open mouth. A staircase sprawled in front of me — *far, far* in front of me — left rugless, polished steps gleaming. A giant chandelier hung far above us. Hundreds of crystals rebounded the light inside, giving the foyer a generous yet faded ambience.

I scanned the innards with wide eyes. "Piss on my head and call me King..."

"What was that, Mr. Graves?"

"It's just Gra..." I trailed off as I noticed how near Jennifer was standing, looking up at me with those sky-blue eyes. She smelled like lavender and flowers and raindrops and kittens... "Mr. Graves it is," I finished with a wolfish grin. She giggled again; my pupils bounced along like happy little rabbits.

Something growled from high above me, at the top of the stairs. The sound was an inhuman rumble, a force of nature. I expected to find a looming spook with hundreds of claws and a toxic, whipping tongue... not a pair of buff dudes wearing only tidy-whities. They were studded with muscle, thighs and arms and chests bulging like plastic bags filled with rocks. The light bounced from their oiled, spray-tanned skin in brilliant rays. I had to squint just facing the twin giants.

"Jenny," one monster grumbled, "who's this guy?"

"This is Graves! He's here to deal with all that moaning that's been coming from underneath the mansion."

The other orc let out a booming chuckle. "I hope that he can tell between that *ghost's* moaning and *your* moaning, Jenny." He smiled at that, real proud of his stupid joke.

"Oh, you guys," Jennifer replied. She shook her head at them like a disappointed mother, fists planted on barely-covered hips. "Run back up to the bedroom, now. I'll meet you up there in a bit. Oil yourselves up while you wait."

"Yes, ma'am!" one yelled. The other clapped his hands quickly, and they both ran off chittering like excited kids.

She giggled again and turned back towards me. "Well, the moaning is coming from the kitchen a few rooms over. Do you think you'll need help finding it, Mr. Graves—"

"It's just Graves," I spat, spinning and stomping in the direction she'd indicated.

I really didn't want to snap at her, but... Christ above, I needed to get laid. It'd been a good few months for good ol' Graves.

Whatever, I thought. *Let's just get this shit over with.*

Jennifer's kitchen was better lit than the foyer; she must have had someone come in and rig up a more modern setup, as the twin beams of light that ran across the entire room's length didn't come from anywhere *close* to the 1940s. Stark light caressed every inch of the black countertop, black cupboards, and black tile that made up the kitchen. The two shades contrasted so fiercely that staring into the room was disorienting in and of itself. An island stretched through the center of the room, black-topped save for a small smudge of white. Moving closer, I rubbed my finger across the smudge and made a smooth trail of darkness visible. I knew better than to taste or smell the white powder, so I rubbed it off on my pant leg.

Mounds of the stuff were piled on the opposite countertop.

I would've packed up, deemed this a simple case of drug-induced hallucinations, and left right then, but the death hum was even *louder* than it'd been outside. Its force was almost palpable, rocking against me in a steady thrum of wails. No wonder Jennifer and her boys could hear the moaning; it was downright *cacophonous.* And it was coming from directly in front of me, inside of the island.

A sink was set into the middle of the countertop, and under that was a cabinet through which its piping could be easily reached. I opened the cabinet and noted the lack of cleaning supplies — something about stones and glass houses tried to squirt into my mind, but I squished it like the pathetic fuckin' bug it was. The hum grew louder even after the short distance I'd crouched, and louder still as I brought my head towards the wooden bottom of the cabinet.

I knocked on the pipes, seeing what my senses would pick up. They were average. Nothing special from the inner walls of the island, either. The floor of the cabinet, though, sounded conspicuously hollow. I looked behind me, checking the coast, then I reeled back and punched the wood, cracking it. I pried back one piece… shit. Nothing.

This is one of the many problems with modern civilization: You people build up your big houses and your irrigation and your fuckin' *plumbing*, not thinking about the dozens of hiding spots you're providing the *spooks!* They sleep between walls, underneath floors, in pipes, down the toilet bowl, doesn't matter; if there's a place you can't see that's not nature-made, they'll hide there. It sure as shit makes *my* job a trillion times harder.

But that's why I always come prepared.

I pulled my shotgun from its sheath. The stock of the gun is layered in thick steel, so it's heavy as fuck — all but unwieldable for the average human. I cracked it open, made sure the chambers were empty, flicked the safety on, and then grabbed its barrel. I brought it over my head, then swung it downwards with a grunt, using my back and sides to arch the shotgun like a sledgehammer. With a *crack* and a jolt up my arms, a huge chunk of marble broke off, which I kicked out of the way. I lifted the shotgun and swung again.

It was a good workout. The barrel had rubber on one side to help my grip, and the stock was weighted with layers of steel. It made the shotgun double as a concussive weapon, which made it *triple* as a tool for demolition. Maybe about thirty minutes, a hundred swings, and a pair of aching shoulders later, I'd shattered around eight feet of counter into large chunks.

The hum still emanated from below the where the sink... *had* been — I'd tossed it across the room during my hastened work. I went down on my hands and knees and put my ear to the wood — I couldn't have fucking X-ray vision, could I? The moan was surprisingly far away, a distant, rattling sigh. My arms were in the groove of things, like well-oiled gears, so I spun it around and arched the gun above my head, ready to *slam* through the floor and finally see what was what.

"HEY!"

I flinched at the sudden shout, lowering the shotgun slowly to my side. I turned and was greeted by the sight of much, *much* too much skin. One of Jennifer's playthings had come down to check on the noise, and he hadn't bothered to make himself decent. Not even a pair of tighty-whities.

"What the hell do you think you're doing, dude? You…" He trailed off as his eyes lowered to my shotgun. They lingered there, one of his lids twitching.

"See something you like?" I asked. "I know it's bigger than yours. You don't have to be embarrassed."

"I think you should leave," he growled. "I mean it."

"Hey, I came to do a job. So your counter got a little fucked. Your mistress is rich; why do you care?" I reached back to sheathe my shotgun. As I raised the impressive weapon, a spark shined in Beefboy's eye, a shade of emotion I absolutely *hate* to see in civilians.

Panic.

"I said *leave*!" he squealed, running at me with speed disproportionate with his size. Before I could jump out of the way, he slammed into me in a viscous tackle, sending every ounce of breath outta my lungs and lifting my feet clear off the ground. I'm not a small guy — I'm of average male height, yes, but every inch of me is threaded with thick muscle — so that was an impressive feat.

I struggled against his encompassing grip, his arms like twin pythons, but it was useless. "Let go-a me you fuckin' moron!" I yelled. Beefboy went to finish his tackle with a roar, diving towards the bare wood over which the island had once stood. I braced myself for the upcoming slam, knowing that Beefboy had to be nearly 400 pounds of cocaine-fueled muscle. But we didn't slam into the ground...

We went *through* it, our combined weight cracking through the plywood as if it were cardboard. I initially thought that my skeleton had shattered like a bundle of twigs, as the sound was raucous and sharp and sudden. My relief lasted only a second.

Because we'd fallen into open blackness.

I'll admit, that surprised me.

My stomach fell out of my body, disrupted by the sudden lack of visible floor. Around us was only thick darkness. Musty smells assaulted me: rotten weeds, moist earth, eons of dense dust. Me and Beefboy gasped at once. Looking over his massive shoulder, I saw the Beefboy-shaped hole in the ceiling shrinking away like my last hope. Humid wind whipped my hair and face. I realized that eventually we were gonna hit *something*... and if this lummox was still on top of me I'd be mushed into the first vintage of Graves wine.

I reeled back and *headbutted* Beefboy with the curve of my tough skull. His sight was filled with stars, his head wavering back and forth in his dazed state. I shifted my weight and spun us around, hoping to use this ogre's mass to save myself from the upcoming pain.

Hey, it was him or me, right?

After another second, I heard whistling slowly rising in volume as the ground came to greet us. I braced myself against Beefboy as heterosexually as possible, then yelped as we crashed onto something rock-solid... and burst through that, too. It wasn't until after another half-second that we landed on actually solid ground. Breath puffed out of both of us upon impact — I thought I felt something *snap* within Beefboy's heaving chest. His glare was accusatory... until his eyes rolled back in his head. He blacked out with a shudder.

Disoriented, I rolled off of my fleshy airbag. Darkness creeped around me, but a small beam of light shined down and illuminated the room just slightly, streaming through the hole that me and Beefboy had made in the kitchen floor. I'd expected the earth to feel mushy and moist with soil. Instead, my feet scuffed on the grainy but solid texture of concrete. This place was man-made, then.

I was liking this less and fuckin' less.

My flashlight turned on with a tiny squeal and shone on concrete walls, concrete ground, and a shattered concrete ceiling. A thick powder coated everything, what must have been *decades* of dust. It stung my nose with its sour stench. One wall was missing, but a gate made with rusty steel bars slotted perfectly into a pair of rails set into the ceiling and floor. I was in a cell.

In the opposite corner sat a disheveled bed draped in moth-eaten blankets. And on top of that... was a skeleton, black and bare and rotted clean as a dog's bone. Whoever that was had died in their sleep — based on their positioning, most likely from starvation. My mouth twisted as I stared at the emotionless, black-eyed skull.

Maybe I'm not the best detective in the world, I thought, *but methinks we've got our spook.*

And, as if in answer, the droning moan reentered my hearing. The noise was so rattling and throaty and real that I knew it was coming from something physical — sort of. A white-blue light seeped behind me, casting my dim shadow against the wall, across the shadowed husk of the skeleton.

I sighed.

The spook had home-field advantage.

Chapter 6

Confined

It wasn't the ugliest spook I'd ever seen, but he wasn't gonna be winning any beauty pageants neither.

His face was near skeletal; his cheeks were sunken into bowls, his eye sockets could hold water, his lips stretched thinner than noodles. He wore a surprisingly nice jacket with padded shoulders, big buttons studding its center. A few medals were pinned to the left breast, denoting a certain military rank. A captain's hat sat on his head with a small American flag sewn onto its side. This guy wasn't a Nazi.

There was an undulating *whoosh whoosh whoosh* from above me as something spun through the air. Smiling at the dead soldier, I reached up and caught the shotgun with one hand, my finger slipping perfectly over the trigger. As I cracked open the weapon, the metal slots on my legs buzzed energetically. There was a tug at my mind. I mentally chose which bullets to use, and two glowing blue shells *zipped* out of them and into the shotty, leaving streams of pale blue light behind them.

My shotty ain't normal, as you may have gathered. It works in tandem with my mind, which works in tandem with the slots on my jumpsuit's legs, to make reloading quick and simple — a perfect triangle of efficiency.

I snapped the shotty closed and aimed at the spook, who sneered at the weapon with open mockery. Blue-white exploded in front of me with a *pfff.*

Captain Spook looked surprised as the twin shells sunk into his chest and sent him sprawling backwards. He collided with the opposite wall, howling in sudden agony. His blue radiance dimmed, and the spook's milky pale flesh suddenly looked more physical than normal. My shells have that effect on the specters, leaving them open to all sorts of mundane weapons.

Such as my big meaty fist.

I punched Captain Spook in the side of his dumb fuckin' head, feeling a satisfying crunch from his now-physical skull. He shouted, then fell against the wall limply. I went down on one knee next to him.

"Can you talk?"

"Uaaaagh," he groaned. A splash of indignance flashed in a white pupil. He stared at me ruefully behind his shelf-like brow. I gave him a backhanded smack.

"How 'bout now, Casper?"

The spook coughed to the side. "Bl...blyes. Yes. I can talk." His voice had a sort of echoey effect to it, as if he were speaking into a tin can. A deeper version of his voice followed each word in a demonic harmony.

"Should I kill you?" I asked.

"Please… Oh, please don't…" He sounded young.

"You sure? 'Cause I kinda want to."

"No, please... I need to... to stay. Answers... Please."

"Why the hell do you want to stick around *here*?" I said, standing. "This shit hole ain't exactly Heaven, to say nothing of the rest of the living world."

"Answers..." he moaned.

I rolled my eyes. This wasn't the first time I'd met a spook stuck in limbo because of some "unanswered" questions. More often than not, they had their answers, they just didn't like 'em. Denial's one hard stain to wipe out.

It also wasn't my fucking problem.

"So, you won't move on voluntarily?" I asked.

"Yes. I must stay... Answers... need answers."

"Suit yourself, pal." His skeletal face melted into boyish relief as I sheathed the shotgun.

Then stunned horror as I drew Baby, her light filling the small cell and the angelic choir joining with the assaulting hum.

"No... no, *please*."

"Sorry, guy. You're disrupting a date between me and my wallet, and I'm hoping to reach home base by tonight. If you won't leave willingly," I kissed the side of my sword, "Baby's more than willing to persuade you."

I'd expected my scare-tactic to work, for Captain Spook to panic and immediately flee to the Other Side... but he didn't. He stared at me with open hatred, not fear and not panic. He wanted to kill me. He really wanted those fuckin' answers.

"Fine," I snarled, swinging the Blade towards the spook's thin neck, aiming to slice through it like a stalk of celery. Captain Spook *howled* as he saw the quickly moving sword, then shot upwards and out of the way, up and over my head. I turned to face him... but he was gone.

Strange. I would've expected him to go all out — to try his dang darndest to kill me as quickly as possible so he could return to his amazing life of sitting around and moaning 24/7. But he'd vanished.

Beefboy wriggled on the ground in front of me, finally waking up — I'd totally forgotten about the big fucker. Pain-filled groans escaped him as he struggled to stand. He shook and grunted, but eventually he was off the ground, his head drooping and facing the dusty concrete. His breath was ragged and short, streaming alongside pathetically silent whimpers.

"You okay, big guy?" I said. "Did that fall loosen what few screws you had left?"

With a sickening *crack*, Beefboy's head snapped up. Each cheek stretched and bulged, making way for his spreading grin. Drool dribbled through his revealed gums and down his chin. He stared at me with wild eyes... each surrounded by a blue-white mist, both pupils now bluer than an Arion's.

"Oh, you little bitch," I groaned. The Captain laughed, throaty and deep and inhuman.

"What's happening?" he asked, voice suddenly dripping with fear. He sneered at me with malice, crouching and preparing for a thorough tackle. "Dude? Why can't I control my body?" The worried, confused words contrasted with the Captain's expression; an internal battle for control was taking place. Beefboy was still kicking, his emotions strong enough to override some of the Captain's murderous impulses.

But the spook was in full command of the physical, which is all that really matters when you're trying to kill someone.

With a shrill shriek of rage-fear, Captain Beefboy sped towards me. This little bastard knew that I'd avoid hurting a civilian, so he'd possessed Beefboy to gain the upper hand. The Captain was clever... and powerful; it takes a lot of passion and emotional baggage to keep a spook anchored to the physical realm, let alone allow them to actually *possess* someone. I needed to be careful.

"Sorry, Baby," I said as I tossed my sword to the side; Beefboy's death was all but guaranteed if I used the Blade in this fight. I'm not *great* at hand-to-hand, but I thought I could handle this bozo. Regardless of how good at fighting the Captain was in life, he was dealing with probably 150 extra pounds here. I just needed to—

Captain Beefboy punched me in the head so hard that my feet went flying out from under me. I fell to the side, head aching as if it were filled with shards of plastic. Two Captain Beefboys stood above me, teeth bared in a growl. He roared and jumped to deal the final blow. I pictured his knees crushing my rib cage and everything behind it, or his elbow caving my head in like one of those Lindor chocolate balls. All sorts of wonderful imagery like that.

With a gasp, I rolled out of the way. Captain Beefboy collided with the ground and actually fuckin' *cracked* the concrete, his fist puncturing the years-old material and sending pointed shards exploding outwards like an animal's quills.

Fuck, I thought. I hadn't had much of a chance to fight someone possessed. It looked like whatever physical attributes the spook had while they were alive — strength, speed, sight, whatever — *combined* with their host's.

In other words: *ruh-roh.*

"I feel funny," Beefboy groaned, despite his energetically moving body.

My vision corrected itself, and I pulled myself up before Captain Beefboy's next charge. Rushing at me, he screamed a shrill scream, Beefboy still controlling the vocal cords. The pain pulsed in time with my heartbeat and rocked the inside of my head as if it were a gong. But I struggled through it and faced the monster's upcoming attack. I sidestepped his deadly tackle and kicked him in the back as he passed, forcing him roughly onto his stomach. I reached for my shotgun, so I was one-handed when his two feet came up in a horse-buck. My right hand blocked some, but one foot hit me square in the chest and I flew backwards and hit the wall.

Captain Beefboy got to his feet in one move, graceful as a ballerina despite his mountainous stature. Blinded by his rage and howling like a steam engine, he came for another wild attack. I rolled up and whipped out my shotgun, *cracking* it open and instantly loading it with a pair of rubber shells. I aimed at his chest, wanting to incapacitate the Captain without accidentally piercing his eye and killing Beefboy.

He realized what was happening just in time to jump to the side and dodge the spray of rubber. Small spheres bounced around the cement cell, some cutting into my face and arms and embedding into the floor and walls.

"What the *hell,* man!?" Beefboy yelled. Then he shook his head violently, a wild look whipping over his glowing eyes. "*Be quiet,*" the Captain yelled back. Beefboy obliged, the last spark of his will crushed underneath the spook's like an especially bothersome bug. The Captain grinned at me — in full control of his wicked impulses — then roared and dove straight for my waist.

With every ounce of strength I could conjure, I spun the shotgun and cracked the flying behemoth right under the chin in a savage uppercut, using his momentum to counterbalance the shotgun's immense weight like a wooden bat hitting a baseball. Captain Beefboy's momentum stopped completely; he fell out of the air with a new wave of dust.

Catching my breath, I kneeled next to him and touched a finger to his neck — his heart was still beating. I saw his back slightly rise and fall with struggling breaths, letting out a ragged groan with every exhale. The Captain hadn't reappeared, so Beefboy hadn't been totally knocked out, just really disoriented. I grabbed his shoulders and flipped him onto his back with a grunt of effort. His mouth was bloodied — he lethargically spat a pearly white tooth to the side — but other than that there wasn't much damage.

"Lordy Lord," I said. "Whatever am I gonna do with you, ya big lug?"

Almost immediately, he lashed out a muscly claw, reaching for my throat. Captain Beefboy was all tuckered out, though, so I was able to easily dodge and catch his wrist. I bent it at a wrong angle, bones scraping as I did, for which he gifted me an agonized howl.

"Know this, Captain," I said. "I try not to kill civilians — it's surprisingly bad for business — but you are *dangerous*. If I don't end you, you'll most likely go on a rampage, which will more than likely end with Jennifer Nee dead; you're coming between me and my pay." I dropped his wrist. Two average shells flew into the chamber as I cracked the shotty. I pointed it at Captain Beefboy's fat head. "What's it gonna be? You go to the Other Side on your own accord? Or do I get to turn that beautiful face into Mama's mashed potatoes?"

Captain Beefboy glared into my eyes, trying to sniff out a bluff.

All he found was a pair of black-staring shotgun barrels.

"W-wait," he croaked. "You need my help!"

I put my finger over the trigger and tucked the barrel snuggly under his chin.

"How are you going to get out of here without me!" he screamed. "Do you even know where we *are!?*"

"I'll figure it out," I said. "One thing at a time — I've got another box needs tickin'."

Some of the fear leaked out of his eyes, like he *knew* that I'd die without him here. I growled at him. "How the hell could *you* help me anyway? This looks like a prison, and *you're* one of the fuckin' prisoners; I kinda doubt that you'd know your way around here."

"It's not a prison. Me and my squad were sent here for recon, but we got caught. Still, I got a pretty good look at the place before that."

I narrowed my eyes at him, but eased up on the pressure.

As bad as I wanted to blast the stupid bastard's head off... that could always wait. It's not like he'd be able to do much with my gun trained on his back and sword around his neck. It *was* a risk though...

"As you said, I'm dangerous in this guy's body." He nodded his head towards the cell door behind us.

Dammit.

I made a noise, a mix between a sigh and a growl, then stood and holstered the shotty. I reached and helped Captain Beefboy up, struggling with his extraordinary weight even with my strength. He looked at me thankfully, but I kept a firm grip on his wrist.

"You try anything," I spat through gritted teeth, "and you'll be decorating this Nazi's wall." He frowned at me, eyes contemplative and hesitant. "Yeah, not exactly the American Dream," I said.

I let go of his wrist and he walked over to the door. He gave himself some room to build up momentum, then ran at it, shoulder first. The thing popped clean off its railing and out of the cement with a *clang*. It wobbled in midair then fell to the concrete like the lid of a jar.

He turned back towards me and smiled cockily.

Speaking of cock...

"Okay," I said, grimacing, "first thing we need is to find you a pair of fuckin' underwear."

Chapter 7

My Business

The halls of this place were a straight path of mindless monotony. The floor and ceiling were dust-drenched concrete, just like that cell, but here hung the intermittent lightbulb, dead and faded years past; my suit's flashlight was still the only source of illumination. Cells, all the same size, were built into the wall at even intervals. Some were empty, their gates slid open, while piles of bones occupied others. Charlie — which was the Captain's actual name — looked mournful each time we passed one.

"I wonder why they're not here..." he said once.

"They probably didn't care about the mission as much as you did, chief. They were happy to move on — to escape their starvation or torture or whatever was happening here."

He went silent again, which was fine with me.

As we shuffled further down this endless hall, my boots and Charlie's bare feet scuffing on the filthy floor, I spotted out-of-place symbols along the walls. Some were etched into the wall, while most were painted with a brown substance. The symbols were vaguely circular, but they were too faded by age to be any more legible.

Although, the pentagrams were easy enough to recognize.

Nazis were all sorts of terrible, but I always thought Satanist was the one thing they'd stayed away from. Staring at the faded brown scrawls, I decided to ignore this little addition to Jennifer's case. Charlie's moaning was the only part I was being paid to deal with; creepy Nazi shit was outta my paygrade, as far as I was concerned.

That gnat stirred from its dormancy, ready to bite and scrape.

Finally, we reached the end of the hall. Our footsteps rang hollowly around the darkness, a sound that could only come from a much larger room. My flashlight dimly reflected off glass surfaces and objects, the glare reduced by the heaps of dust. I squinted and saw metal tables topped with beakers and glass funnels — things I thought I recognized as chemistry equipment — but I couldn't spot much else.

Suddenly, a loud buzzing came from behind me, then a heavy-duty light fixture above us exploded in brightness. The room was draped in light, my eyes struggling to adjust. Once they did, I saw that Charlie had opened a heavy steel latch on the wall and pressed a large button underneath it.

"How about a little warning," I said, rubbing my eyes.

He ignored me and walked further into the room which, now that it'd been lit, appeared to be some sort of laboratory; there were shelves and tables left neatly around, topped by hundreds of pieces of glassware — which probably had something to do with science... or something — and a few surprisingly advanced tools for surgery. The same symbols I'd seen earlier were painted randomly on the concrete walls, still too faded to make out completely. A giant slab of technological thingies — buttons, switches, little screens, what have you — stood to my right, flush against the wall and drenched in cobwebs and grainy dust.

Charlie gasped when he noticed the wall of electronics. "I've never seen one of these."

"What the fuck is it?" I asked.

He looked at me, surprised. "I figured these would've been

commonplace by now. It's a computer!"

I laughed raucously, which confused him, which made me laugh harder.

After I finished, I noticed some safety equipment hanging on the wall — namely, a pair of pants. I gestured towards them. Charlie picked them up, then flapped them to remove mounds of dust. He recoiled and looked at me.

"Bro, you're fucking dead. What's a little dust?"

Grimacing, he pulled on the pants and finally put the python to rest.

Both of us now definitively secure in our heterosexuality, we studied the centrepiece of the room: A circle of eight glass tubes. Each tube was about as tall as me and had around twice the circumference. A small screen protruded on a stand next to each.

Charlie walked around the tubes, studying each one. He played with the buttons on their panels, trying to probe for their purpose. Finally, one tube swished open, its front half sliding back and cutting the tube in half. Charlie stepped in and looked up and down its contents; from what I could see from there, the bottoms were filled with black ash and warped black lumps. He lifted one of these lumps and studied it for a moment, then let it fall loosely from his fingers. Ash roiled and spread from the lump like thunder clouds; Charlie moved on to the next tube.

"Hey," I said, "do these tubes have something to do with the exit? If not, can we get a fucking move on?"

"Answers…" was all he said, voice muffled by the glass.

I thought about letting the poor idiot search for his "answers," but then I remembered Agatha's cute little nose... and those piercing purple eyes. Baby seemed to tremble with fear in her sheath. I didn't have time for this.

"Alright, buddy, time to go—" Charlie cut me off, sticking

a hand out of the tube and pointing towards a bookcase at the far end of the room. Tattered books covered each shelf, large and wide as any I'd ever seen. I'd read enough mystery novels to know where this was going. Books fell to the dusty floor as I pulled them off one by one. Most were old medical books, but a few had the look of diaries to them. I flipped through one quickly and saw a foreign language crawling along each line — Latin, I think. Shrugging, I went back to my work.

Finally, one book gave some resistance, then *clicked* mechanically. The shelf next to this one rocked in place. It slid over slowly, covering the now emptied shelf and revealing a sparsely lit staircase, spiraling out of view. *Perfect,* I thought. *I've got my way out. Now I just need to Sever Charlie and collect my pay.*

The door of another tube *whooshed* open behind me. I rolled my eyes and said, "Alright, end of the road, buddy. I've got some important shit to do. Time to go."

He ignored me, crouching and picking something up from the black ash. It was a rounded lump, squeezed between hands so hard it might crack. Beefboy's massive shoulders shook as Charlie sobbed, his monstrous yet saddened voice reverberating from the tube and echoing around the abandoned lab.

"Hey, pal. Time's up—" Charlie stood quickly and *howled* towards the cracked ceiling, ghostly vocal cords shaking the glassware behind me and even the very walls encasing us. I covered my ears and backed away. Beefboy's throat bulged as Charlie roared, his voice melting away and becoming something inhuman, primal, and panicked. Blue-white oozed from the man's bronze skin and mouth and eyes. It fuzzed and coalesced into Charlie's spectral form; sunken eye-sockets stretched as he screamed. Beefboy's body flopped to the ground.

I drew Baby.

Charlie's howling was so powerful that I physically struggled to make my way towards him. "I gotta punch your ticket!" I yelled over the assaulting noise. He kept howling like he hadn't heard me. The noise stretched and distorted, as did Charlie himself; he warped like he was in a funhouse mirror, then faded like smoke. Before I could even make an attempt at Severing him, Charlie *exploded* into quickly dissipating mist. It lingered for a bit, then faded completely. His ghostly shriek still reverberated around the room for seconds after he'd vanished.

"Jesus," I said. My ears rang like car alarms.

I walked over to where Charlie had just been, crouching and peering at the charred bits that he'd been studying before he Severed himself. At the bottom of the tube was a rounded, misshapen pelvis — or what *had* been a pelvis; it was distorted, now oblong and asymmetrical. Bits of the bone had melted like wax, covering the holes where various muscles and organs would've fed through. Other bones were piled around it, so fused and blackened that nothing natural could have killed their original owner.

In the center sat a skull. It stared at me with sightless, twisted eyes. The sockets were twice as large as normal, a shelf of a brow shading them. Teeth stabbed out randomly from its maw, most sharp as a nail. The jaw itself was nearly unhinged. The entire skull was lumped with randomly added layers of bone. On one temple, there was a metal plate attached by thick screws. Faded lightning bolts were etched into the dusty steel.

Hrm, I thought. *This is awfully strange.*

I mean, laboratories under a years-dead Nazi's mansion? Filled with charred, misshapen bones inside of tubes straight out of Star Trek Wars or whatever old sci-fi movie? Satanic imagery painted on the walls and diaries filled with some ancient language? It didn't take the Hardy Boys to tell this was a good ol' mystery in the making. I'm sure those guys would've been drooling like hounds if they got a whiff of this case...

But I ain't Sherlock Holmes, or Nancy Drew — and I sure as shit ain't a fucking *Hardy Boy*. As far as I was concerned, the moaning was done, Charlie had passed on to the Other Side, and my hands were clean. Time to get paid and forget everything I'd seen.

Idly — deep, *deep* in the recesses of my mind — I realized that the death hum was still droning like a foghorn. *Not my fuckin' problem,* I thought, standing and dropping the charred skull. *Let sleeping spooks lie, for now. They want me to come back? Fine. But I ain't doing it for free.*

Oh, poor, poor, simple Graves. Stupid fuckin' idiot Graves.

A second moan joined the hum, this one undulating and choked and struggling behind me. I turned towards it quickly, ready to strike down whatever spook had shown its ugly mug. But it wasn't a spook.

It was Beefboy. He shook and seized on the dusty concrete, spittle foaming and leaking from the corners of his mouth. His eyes rolled back, revealing sickly red veins. Coughing, Beefboy spewed a quick splash of foam, moan vibrating alongside his struggling form.

Okay, that *was* my fuckin' problem.

Chapter 8

Payment

Godamn stupid ghost fucking idiot bitch," I said as I beat on Beefboy's chest. I didn't know CPR, so I was trying to recreate what I'd seen on shows. Didn't work, but eventually, Beefboy's seizure subsided. His muscles stopped twitching, but his eyes stayed open, staring into nothing. He still had a pulse, and was still breathing, so I didn't know what the fuck was happening.

If Beefboy died, this case would get a whole lot stickier. Police would *have* to be involved, meaning a lot more paperwork and a lot more time and a lot more me being killed by a demi-goddess from Hell. They'd probably discover the heavy drug use — oh, and the fucking secret Nazi laboratory, not to mention the blackened skeletons — which would rip this case right out of my hand. Bye-bye, money.

The shittiest part was that I'd technically *solved* the case — the moaning had stopped, the spook had been dealt with — but that wouldn't matter if the regular police got involved. The Union would wipe the case from its records completely. They'd do pretty much anything to stay as far from the normal government as possible, including leaving a respectable hunter — such as myself — unpaid. I wouldn't be allowed to accept *any* money from Jennifer.

The way I saw it, I had one option: ambulance. I'd have to drag this massive idiot up the staircase and drop him in the kitchen, nearby the smudges of used cocaine. I was positive Beefboy had coke in his system; most likely not enough to constitute an overdose, but definitely enough for the doctors to jump to a conclusion and move on to the next bag of money. Plus, because of the Good Samaritan law, they couldn't come and investigate the mansion without further evidence. Sure, he and Jennifer could still be prosecuted — but, hey, she's fuckin' rich. And white! God, I love the rural U.S.! I'm the goodest Samaritan there ever was!

I had a plan, I just needed to execute it.

My breath came ragged as I dragged Beefboy up the never-ending stairs. He bumped along each step, groaning and grunting under his breath, but I thought the bruises would only add to the cover story. Besides, fuck this guy for getting me into this mess in the first place.

We reached the top of the staircase and were greeted by a wooden ceiling. The outline of the trapdoor was barely visible — I would've probably missed it had it not been for the hunk of metal latching it shut from this side. I undid the latch, then pushed open the heavy wooden door. Sunlight burned my eyes as I dragged Beefboy up and into one of the mansion's many hallways; we'd made it above ground level. The stairs continued upwards into what I figured was one of the towers attached to the front of the mansion. We were like twenty rooms away from the foyer, a long-ass way to drag a massive body.

Beefboy's skin squeaked against the black marble as I dragged him through the hall, into the dark foyer, and towards the kitchen. At the bottom of the looming stairs, I imagined what it would look like if his clone came down to greet us.

"What the fucking fuck?" he'd say, or something around as eloquent. He would try something stupid, and I'd more than likely kill him.

I hastened my dragging a little.

Panting, sweat beading on my forehead, I dropped Beefboy to the kitchen's floor, near the smudges of white. I rubbed one of his fingers in the stuff for added effect, letting it limply drag along the counter and fall next to him.

"911, what's your emergency?" the operator asked through the speakers of my shitty flip phone.

"My... friend is overdosing," I replied, too exhausted to try and sell the line. I gave them the address and hung up.

After taking a few seconds to catch my breath and gather my thoughts, I stood and acted casual. Within five minutes, blue and red lights seeped through and refracted off the windows in the kitchen. Wood creaked as the front door was thrown open, followed by boots and wheels squeaking on the marble. A pair of paramedics walked in with a stretcher. They looked at Beefboy nonchalantly, then at me, raising eyebrows.

"His first time with the stuff," I said, my thoughts still a little fuzzy from exhaustion. "He was just experimenting. I'm clean and sober."

The paramedics' brows raised higher. They gestured towards the mounds of cocaine littering the kitchen like kitty litter. Too tired to come up with a convincing argument, I simply stared at them silently, revealing no emotions. They looked back... then broke the stare; people might fight back against outright aggression, or take advantage of kindness, but they usually won't try to budge someone neutral. It's not worth trying to push a boulder out of the way when you can just walk around it.

Through a lot of sweat, grunting, and even roaring from effort, the paramedics lifted Beefboy and place him, crashing, on the stretcher. The wheels *screamed* as the great lummox was wheeled out of the mansion. The paramedics just managed to heft him into the ambulance, I saw through the window, and looked relieved and even surprised at what they'd accomplished.

There was another person standing near them: A fit, subtly muscular woman wearing tight-fitting denim pants, a buttoned plaid long sleeve, and a sturdy pair of boots. Her lips were as plump as pears, and her hips were wide and succulcnt cnough to makc my mouth water, but she was decidedly more masculine than your average lady; her hair was short, a dirty blonde cowlick, and her cheekbones were rough and angular. A golden crucifix fell over her small breasts, swinging from a golden chain.

Aubrey Cohen. Shit.

Me and Aubrey weren't exactly friends. She was a detective in the Hartsville Police Department — i.e., a cop. We'd butted heads on a few occasions, usually because she refused to accept the existence of the Other Side and its inhabitants — meaning I was normally the one *actually* solving the case, while she scratched her head, wondering why that assaulter could possibly fear garlic and holy water. She's a fine detective, I've heard, but her ignorance of the Other Side limits her abilities. Blame it on Catholicism, I guess.

More prudent for now, a cop was here. I needed to play this *real* fuckin' smooth. Even if she has her blinders up when it comes to the supernatural, Aubrey's no slouch.

Her heavy combat boots clunked on the marble as she entered the kitchen. The cop's eyes went first to Mount Coke, then they focused on me in all their green fury. She clenched her tough jaw, visibly restraining herself from balling her fists at her sides like a little girl.

"Fucking knew it," the cop growled.

"Aubrey!" I exclaimed. "Radiant as always." She

clenched even harder at the use of her first name. I swear, Miss Aubrey Cohen seems to *hate* being reminded that she's a lady. But, despite the muscular stature and boyish haircut, that's what she still claims to be.

And honestly... I'm kinda into it. The way she subtly swings her hips and purses her pillowy lips in thought contrasts so nicely with her more masculine attributes. She's attractive in a way that few women are.

"Shut the fuck up, Graves, you stupid piece of shit," she spat through gritted teeth.

"My lady!" I put my hand to my chest in mock offense. "Such language!"

Aubrey strode forward and stood in front of me, glaring up and into my eyes. She's a few inches shorter than me, which I *know* eats away at her insides. "What the hell's going on here," she said, more a demand than a question.

"Me and some... ah... bros were hanging out and... drinking beer, when—"

"Graves, for once, just don't be an asshole."

I laughed. "I'm usually pretty nice to *cops*—" I leaned down and squinted at her chest, pointing out her missing badge "—which it looks like you're not today. Some off-duty investigating, Aubrey? Tsk, tsk."

She kept glaring, green eyes blazing.

"I know how badly you want the chief's gig," I said, "but you're *way* out of your damn league here. All you'd do is embarrass yourself — which I'd be all fuckin' for, honestly, if you wouldn't *also* get in the way of *my* work."

"Who's the elephant?" she asked, ignoring me and nodding towards the ambulance.

"My identical twin brother."

Aubrey rolled her eyes then turned to leave. I stoically observed her hips and ass, perfectly toned and as round as a pair of freshly baked cakes, hugged tightly by her jeans. When she got to the exit of the kitchen, she said, "Keep staring, Graves. You'll be watching this ass from a prison cell if you're hiding anything from me. I know something's not right here, and I'll be damned if you get to the bottom of it before I do." Looking over her shoulder, she showed me a small grin. "I've got all the time in the world."

What did that mean? There was a sense of bitterness when she said it, like she'd be wronged somehow… or that she'd been canned. Yikes. Aubrey was a loose cannon; knowing her, that meant she was *desperate* for her job back. She'd scour Jennifer Nee's mansion until she found anything even *resembling* a lead, so I needed to collect my pay ASAP.

Aubrey was still smiling at me through the kitchen's window as she ducked into her dinky silver Camry. I frowned and waited for her and the ambulance to drive down the hill and out of sight, then walked into the foyer, facing the grey shadows at the top of the stairs.

The upstairs was no less lavish than the rest of the mansion, of course, so I had some issues finding my way around. The few rooms I opened were empty, filled only by the evening's dwindling sunlight, streaming through giant windows that made up one side of the black marble cube.

After a few minutes of hopeless searching, I heard another moan come from a couple of hallways away — though this was the *good* kind of moaning; clearly Beefboy Two and Jennifer were still going at it. I hated to cock-block Jennifer — I guess "muff-rebuff" might be more accurate in this case — but I *really* hated working for free. Using the sounds of her rhythmic moaning, and the eventual creaking of her bed frame, I triangulated her location.

Graves need sex, I thought, listening to the melody of her ecstasy through her bedroom door. I knocked on the door.

Jennifer's throaty moans and the squeaking, rocking of the bedframe didn't stop, so I knocked harder.

"Ms. Nee, I've taken care of your spook. I'm in a bit of a rush, so it'd be great if you could... *complete* this later so we can finish this transaction."

No change. I tried the doorknob, but it resisted me stiffly. Fine.

I reared up my leg — readying my specialized third-person contraceptive — then kicked the door down in one. Jennifer gasped as it came crashing into her room. I stepped in, looking through the room's giant window to conserve *any* semblance of professionalism...

The beasts still didn't stop!

"All right, fuck this," I said, turning towards them. Jennifer and her toy were attached like pieces of sticky Velcro; her legs were wrapped around his hips, her red nails clawed into his broad back, their hips writhed as if they were made of rubber.

Graves need sex. NOW.

I shook my head and approached the pair, neither of whom had noticed my presence.

"Jennifer, the sooner you pay up, the sooner I'm outta here. Please."

"Oh! Um. Sorry, Mr. Graves," she said through pants. "This guy's got more horsepower than usual! And that's saying something. Can you come back tomorrow—" She was cut off by an especially enthusiastic thrust, her sudden moan piercing and raw.

"No, I can't. It will only take a second." I looked directly at the guy. "Can you give it a rest, dude? She's not fuckin' going anywhere."

No response and no "giving it a rest."

I pulled him off Jennifer while keeping my eyes strictly on

the ceiling. He fell to the ground with a thud, panting loudly. "Go get a swig of Gatorade or something, champ. It's halftime…" I trailed off as I noticed something off, yet familiar, about him.

His eyes glowed a radiant white-blue.

This was gonna get old real fuckin' fast.

Beefboy Two — henceforth called Beef*man* — made an inhuman gurgling sound in the back of his throat. His eyes were overcast, distant, unfocused, yet I got a sense of animosity from him. Whatever had possessed Beefman was much less human than Charlie; he lacked any sign of the previous host's personality or feeling. Even if Beefman was a strong guy, he apparently wasn't strong enough to emotionally overcome whatever had gotten inside of him. His look and demeanor had an almost feral cast to them, like a stray dog backed into a corner.

A stray dog at full mast.

"Hey, hey now. Settle down," I said. "Why are you here, guy? Just trying to get some action? Believe me when I tell you the Other Side has plenty of it."

Beefman's eyes and limbs twitched randomly. I had trouble predicting his next move, as he didn't seem to be thinking about much — he had no tells. There was one thing on his mind... and it was attached to the person sitting on the bed behind me.

Realizing that, my right arm bent reflexively to grab Baby's hilt. Beefman let out a guttural yell in response, a defiant roar that had no place coming from a human's throat. Jennifer squeaked a girlish scream as Beefman barreled forward.

I drew Baby and pointed it forward so Beefman would run into her if he came too close. It wouldn't be easy to bat the sword out of the way, so I wanted Beefman to have to stop in his tracks or completely avoid me. We locked eyes — mine calm and prepared, his wide with bestial rage — and I readied myself for Beefman's dodge…

Baby plunged right through his stomach.

Jennifer screeched.

My mouth fell open. Baby had entered and exited Beefman as cleanly as a knife through steak. He loomed over me, Baby's hilt flush with his abs. Even this close to him I could see her red-drenched blade jutting out of his back, dripping bits of viscera and stringy blood. Small ropes of entrails protruded from where she'd bit. My hands were immediately doused in slippery, warm crimson.

I tried to gather my thoughts, to develop a plan: What would happen to Beefman's body? What about the cops? How could I explain to Aubrey? Most importantly, would I still be getting paid?

I went through all that shit with Beefboy just for this dumbass to kebab himself like a big chunk of barbecued pineapple.

Beefman growled at me, interrupting my thoughts. He glared, surprisingly cognizant for a guy with five feet of greatsword churning up his insides, then coughed blood in my face. I recoiled, releasing Baby's hilt, then fell onto the floor. Wiping blood out of my eyes, I heard the disgusting squishing noises of Beefman pulling Baby out of his stomach. Bits of organ and streams of burgundy blood fell out with her, leaving a writhing slit in Beefman's abdomen.

Which then sewed itself together. Blue mist shrouded the wound, caressing each side of the gash until it healed.

That's a new one.

Beefman dropped Baby on the ground and sneered at me. I elected to leave my Blade where she was for now. If she couldn't send this spook to the Other Side with a stab through its host's gut, I'd have to make said host... obsolete.

Permanently.

Sorry, Beefman, but rubber bullets wouldn't be any help this time.

Before I could even touch the shotty's stock, though, Beefman was in front of me. He grabbed the front of my jumpsuit and effortlessly lifted me off the floor. Panicking, I kicked wildly, aiming for his bare nuts. I landed a solid hit, but Beefman didn't seem to notice. My blows thudded against his tough skin and bounced off like nothing. He held me like a momma cat holds her kitten, growling as I feebly struggled against his immovable fists.

With a roar, he spun me around, pivoting on his heel. I yelled as we danced, getting sick to my stomach. The world melted into blurred paintings. Beefman swiveled his arms…

And chucked me towards the fuckin' window.

With a *crash*, I slammed through the glass like piss through paper. The setting sun's light blinded me as I flew into the open. My stomach roiled. Jennifer's screams danced along the wind rushing through my ears and whipping my hair. Trees and their sharp branches came to meet me like old lovers.

I hit the ground, shoulder first.

And passed out.

Chapter 9

Scenarios

I dreamed that Agatha had gotten her way, that she'd hunted me to the far ends of this realm like some feral animal. When she found me, shaking and afraid and naked other than the Blade of Balance, she shrieked in triumph and went for the kill. She unsheathed her broadsword and touched it to the side of my head. Tiny jade-green pupils stared down at me in fury. The sword's point *jabbed* into my temple like a toothpick through a peach, then came out, then went back in, then out...

The sword chirped at me.

Cracking open my eyes, I saw a little blue bird hopping next to my head excitedly, fallen orange leaves cracking underneath its feet. Chirping once, it pecked me again with its pointed black beak. I growled and swatted it away.

Based on the shadows of the looming trees rising around me, a few hours had passed since the sun's crest. I'd been asleep for hours... *hours!* I did not have that kinda fucking time.

That four-story fall may have just secured my death.

I stood, definitely not panicking, the cold biting at my nose like a stubborn partner. I reached for Baby, who could provide me with some needed warmth.

Fuck. She was still in Jennifer's bedroom.

Groaning, I left the little forest and went into the mansion.

I was *not* excited to see whatever was left in Jennifer's room. Gruesome images flashed through my head: Jennifer's gored corpse left battered and bloodied on the bed; Beefman sitting in waiting, ready to bisect me with his bare hands; Baby snapped in two, her light drained and her life forfeit. I nearly cried at thinking of that, even knowing she couldn't be broken — at least not by someone with less than god-level strength.

Shit, I thought, *I've got no idea how strong Beefman is. For all I know, he could be powerful enough to break Baby like a twig...*

I hastened my step.

In contrast to those vivid images, the bedroom was mostly how I, ah, *left* it. The bedspread was in disarray, Beefman's blood and bits of organ stained the red carpet, the autumn breeze howled through the broken window, crisp and chill. A few things were missing, though — namely, Jennifer and Beefman. That wasn't good.

Even worse, Baby was gone. Now *that* was downright earth-shattering. If she got into the wrong hands...

I couldn't consider that. Not yet. First, I needed to hunt Beefman and Jennifer down. If she were dead, that wouldn't look great for good ol' Graves. Call it a permanent stain on my record or a slap on the wrist, the result was the same: Moths meet wallet.

Plus, Jennifer was, in a way, under *my* protection. If I couldn't help her, what did that say about my skill as a ghost hunter? When Earth has a stroke of shit luck and a solar flare turns all of your family to ash — or, more realistically, when you drown screaming about how you should've switched to a Hybrid — one truth will remain unquestionable: Graves gets the job done.

The hum was still droning in my peripheral hearing, albeit

noticeably far away. That wasn't gonna be much help. The spook was still definitely in the mansion, though. Even a spook that can possess someone mid-coitus and heal fatal wounds wouldn't usually leave its haunt. Essentially, they'd have to find the satisfaction they'd been missing at their death, then *still* decide to remain in this realm. Very few spooks did that, and those that did mutated and lost all control, becoming something entirely different. Beefman didn't seem the kind of spook to suddenly be satisfied with all the fucking he was doing, so I doubted that was it.

I'm normally able to suss out the location of a spook using just the hum and Baby's tells, but clearly Jennifer's mansion wasn't your average locale — meaning the place was fuckin' huge. Only the hum was evident, and I could possibly spend *hours* — which I didn't have if I wanted to keep Ms. Nee (and myself) alive — just on the *chance* that I'd pick something up. I needed a different method of hunting. Something that I'd really been trying to avoid.

I needed a medium.

I needed Gus Beuzzle.

Goddamnit, I thought, leaving the messy bedroom.

As I strolled down the hill and towards the Specter Detector's base, I gathered the day's many events.

Jennifer Nee had heard moaning coming from underneath her mansion, made by a dead American soldier, imprisoned and presumably starved to death by the Nazi who used to own the mansion, Erick Horst. Charlie must've been mindlessly expressing his regrets through spooky noises — regrets strong enough to push him into possessing a civilian and confronting me — but I still had no idea what those regrets were. I assumed they had something to do with the warped bones that he'd found in the Nazi's lab, which brought a whole separate slew of questions. Either way, I was sure those remains were related to whatever had possessed Beefman, thus the rest of this case.

Aubrey Cohen was sure to be snooping around Jennifer's mansion now, which meant that I'd have to be extra careful; if she saw the very real danger that Jenny was in, she'd have the right to report the case and take over before I could sneeze. I was the only one with the connections, experience, and equipment needed to save Jennifer, so I couldn't let that happen. Or I wouldn't get paid.

Now, Jennifer had been kidnapped by a possessed beefcake and carried deeper into her endlessly gigantic mansion. I needed... I wouldn't say *help,* per se — a *servant* would be the right term, I think. I needed a servant to sniff out her location; Gus Beuzzle was that servant.

Oh and, can't forget, I still needed to find a host for Agatha, lest my soul be Severed from my body and Baby stripped away from me. I'd really hoped to have this case wrapped up by now — Josephi would've finally been outta my hair, and I would've been able to focus on finding someone with a more twisted heart than mine.

I still had a day and some change. That would have to be enough.

The Specter Detectors' HQ was about what I expected: A one story suburban home with beige walls and burgundy shingles flowing over each other on its roof. A little concrete driveway led to a small garage, door rolled all the way up. Beuzzle's big van was parked by the curb out front. A cute blue Sedan sat next to it.

Shelves lined the inside of the garage, covered in ghost hunting equipment: spirit boxes, infrared cameras, EMF readers, that kinda shit. Beuzzle tinkered with something on an impressive workbench draped with blueprints and files.

As I strolled up, I heard pop music playing from speakers hanging around the small workspace. Beuzzle mouthed the words and swayed his body to the rhythm.

Kill me.

I stopped just outside, a few feet in front of Beuzzle's workbench. He didn't notice me standing there, so I cleared my throat loudly. He didn't hear.

"*Beuzzle*," I said. He kept swinging his hips, just slightly too sensual. Jennifer Nee sang through the speakers: *Ravish me. Use me. Love me. Abuse me.* He gyrated and thrust with each rhyme.

"Beuzzle, for fuck's sake! Kids *play* around here!"

He yelled and fell on his ass, cheeks and chin jiggling. I looked at him and pointed my index finger towards the ground. "Turn Jenny down." He rushed to grab a little remote on his workbench, then shut the music off.

"Graves! What are *you* doing here?" Abruptly, a stupid smile spread across his face like butter on a pale loaf of bread. "Are *you* a fan of Jennifer Nee too!?"

"No," I answered instantly. "I'm just, uh, working a case for her right now, is all. She rehearses sometimes."

"You're working for *Jennifer* flipping *Nee*? Holy crap! How'd you land *that* job?"

"Josephi. How the fuck else?"

Suddenly, Beuzzle's chubby face curdled as if it were ancient sour cream. "That rat," he growled — well, more of a grumble, like a little bear cub. "That filthy rat! We had a deal! Any and all of his jobs were supposed to..." His voice trailed off. It looked like he'd forgotten I was there.

"A deal, huh?" I grinned and took a few steps forward. "Sounds mighty interesting, Gus, my boy."

He flinched. "N-no. Very *not* interesting, actually. I-it's in the past, anyhow. You don't have to worry about it."

"Oh, I'm sure I do." I stopped in front of his workbench. "If Josephi is involved with anything, I generally assume that it will eventually come back to tear at my ass like a rabid dog." I calmly laid my hands on the table, leaning forward. "You're not protected by the Union this time, Gussy-poo, so I'd recommend cooperation."

I let my words hang in silence. Light sheened off the sweat on Beuzzle's face.

"F-fine," he squeaked eventually, resigned. "Josephi came to me a few days ago, soon after your, uh, *incident* at that other job." I winced at that, but nodded in understanding. "The other members of my group had... *split* with me by then, so I was alone and desperate for work. Heck, I thought of quitting hunting altogether."

"What convinced you otherwise?"

"He offered Mallery's case. It sounded like something I could take."

"That's it?" I asked, crossing my arms. "What was so special about her case?"

He looked at me with big doe eyes and bit his wobbling lip.

"Christ, Beuzzle. Just spit it the fuck out."

"Josephi said that, uh... *you* would be willing to take the case with me. He said that maybe we'd be partners..."

"Oh, merciful Lord."

"Still, that wasn't quite enough to convince me. Josephi also told me he'd help boost my career after Mallery's problem was solved, by giving me all the best jobs before showing them to anyone else."

My teeth ground together hard enough to make bread. Beuzzle gained a ponderous look. "Hm. What are you doing here anyway, Graves?'

"That fucking bastard," I growled silently.

"What was that?"

"We got fucking played, kid. I'll wring that little piece of shit's neck until his fucking eyeballs pop out."

"What do you mean? What did Josephi do?"

"*He set us up, that's what*," I roared, turning back towards him. "He orchestrated Mallery and Jennifer's cases so that I'd *have* to take them."

"Why would he do that?"

"I've got no fucking clue, goddamn it!"

Beuzzle flinched but said, "And why involve *me*? Josephi seems to have it out for you, but..."

"Probably just to torture me," I said.

He wilted at that. I sighed. It wasn't the kid's fault he was involved, nor was it his fault he could be a fuckin' dweeb. I needed his help; even if that's what Josephi wanted — for whatever reason — it was still a fact.

"Look, Beuzzle," I said, swallowing my pride, "I came here to ask for your help. Jennifer's haunt is gigantic, and I need someone with a little more precision to help me find its spook."

I expected Beuzzle to fall upon his chubby knees and praise me like the god I was, but instead, he frowned. "I don't know..." he mumbled.

"Huh? What the fuck don't you know? It's Jennifer Nee, kid. Weren't you just violating the air to her music?" He averted eye contact, staring at the ceiling and thinking, considering. "Didn't you want to be partners with me or some shit?"

"I'm just a little busy right now, Graves."

Before I could argue, a woman's voice echoed through the garage, streaming through an open door. "Gus, are you finished yet?"

"Almost, Jessie," he replied, looking down at what he'd been working on earlier. Now that I was closer, I saw what it was: A heap of colored wires neatly tied together, strung between a metal box and a metal plate, with a glass bulb bulging from it. "Just needs a few little tweaks and then I'll... leave." Beuzzle choked like he was on the verge of tears.

The woman peeked her head into the garage. Curly brown hair fell to her shoulders, matched by dark skin splattered by darker freckles. She wore horn-rimmed glasses, complete with a chain attaching both temple tips so she'd be able to remove the glasses and let them hang around her neck like a librarian. She wasn't much older than Beuzzle.

"It doesn't have to be this way," she said, ignoring me. "I want to be *friends*, Gus. Just because it didn't work between us doesn't mean the Specter Detectors are out of commission! What are me and Em going to do without you?"

Beuzzle grimaced at the last sentence, then spun to face Jessie. "I'm sure that you and 'Em' have *plenty* to do without me," he said, a sudden fiery rage sparking inside the chubby teenager. "In fact, I'm pretty sure you were both able to do a *whole lot* without me — y'know, your frickin' *boyfriend*."

Jessie shut up at that, looking to the side and blushing lightly. Gus glared at her, then gestured towards me. "Besides, me and Graves just picked up a new case. We'll take the van up to Jennifer Nee's mansion and be out of your hair, if I'm such a friggin' *bother*."

"Jennifer Nee?!" Jessie yelled. "How did you—"

Gus put his pudgy finger up, cutting her off. "Sorry, Jess. This case is on a need-to-know basis. C'mon Graves, Jenny's waiting for us."

You little devil, I thought. I could tell he relished in Jessie's shock, even if he didn't look at her as we strolled towards his goofy white van.

"I'm sure you're wondering what that was about," Beuzzle asked as he drove. His van looked and smelled surprisingly clean. Tools and electronics rattled in the back with each bump.

"Not really," I replied.

"Well, Jessie... she..." Beuzzle's eyes glazed over, moisture pooling underneath their bottom lids.

"Dude, are you—"

He suddenly slammed his fists on the steering wheel and yelled, "*She cheated on me!*"

"Woah there, big guy!" I said. "Relax and look at the road."

"With that *amateur.*" He veered hard to the right, tires screeching like banshees. I rammed into the door, tools crashed and clanged behind us. "*Em,*" he said mockingly. "Those two couldn't *detect* a freaking *specter* if it flew right up their butts!"

"Uh, is Em the guy that Jessie banged behind your back?" I asked in an attempt to calm him down.

He looked at me, his face scrunched up in anger and confusion. "Em — Emily — is a lady. And they didn't... bang." He returned to his default state of shivering and whining. "At least not *yet*."

Yeesh. Teen drama. That's something I'm glad I missed in my youth.

"Okay, so if they didn't fuck, what the hell's the matter?"

"That case... the one that you... well, y'know."

"The one you three took over? Over at the Garcias' place?"

"The same." Beuzzle's hands squeaked as he gripped the leather wheel. "Those two... they kicked me off the job. Em said that I 'wasn't needed.' That I'd only get in the way." He gave a disdainful laugh. "Can you imagine? Brains, muscle, and nothing to back them up? Spector minus the detector? Well, *that's* what they did."

I didn't reply, unsure of what to say or if I cared enough to continue humoring him.

"Jessie just thinks Emily's so *cool*," he growled after a silence. "'Oh, look at me. I Severed a few ghosts.' Whoop-dee-freaking-doo. Emily wouldn't have been able to Sever *anything* if *I* hadn't found it first."

"So, Emily's the scythe in your group, huh?"

"She tries to be," Beuzzle replied, "but she's new. Still, I've got to admit that she's taken to the practice impressively quickly." He grimaced. "That's why Jessie thinks she's some knight in shining armor or something. What am I? Just the geek with the walkie-talkie?"

Yes, I thought. But I said, "Hey, now's your chance to prove them wrong, ain't it?"

He frowned. "I'm still not sure about this gig, Graves."

"The fuck you mean? We're already almost to Jennifer's mansion!"

"I was hoping to, you know, show up at the Garcias' haunt and show the girls what for... unless you'd like to help me...?"

"Oh, you can fuck right off," I laughed. "I've got plenty on my plate already."

Beuzzle bit his lip. "What if... what if I work for free? You can have 100% of the pay for this case."

You mangey fuck, I thought. Two scenarios flashed in my head: In one, Agatha had stolen Baby from me. She polished the Blade with my bare skull, sharpening it to a deadly point. Her sights were dead on Hartsville and all of its innocent, vulnerable souls...

The other was of me diving headfirst into a big pile of treasure, larger than Smaug's hoard. I breached the tide of gold like the ocean's surface, spitting out shining coins and gleaming gems as if they were water. Jennifer Nee waited deep within the hoard's depths, breasts bare and legs splayed...

"I have to say, after *we* — the Specter Detectors — had to take over for *you*, Graves… things really fell apart." He stared through the window, head still.

I glared at him. My track record as a ghost hunter had been flawless, as unblemished as a baby's ass – *had* been. That is, until the Garcia case…

That's one pimple that could use popping, I guess.

"So?" Beuzzle interjected. "What do you say?"

"Give me 30% of the Garcia gig, and you've got a deal. And we have to go to Jennifer's first. There's, uh, something pressing I have to take care of."

Beuzzle smiled. "It's a plan!"

As we neared Jennifer's mansion, the sun steadily dipped towards its resting place, approaching nightfall and the end of my first day. I heard a big grandfather clock *a-tick a-tocking* inside my head, marching along with my heartbeat, possibly pumping its last spurts of lifeblood.

Beuzzle ranted and raved about his partners — about their lack of respect for him and his prowess as a hunter. I half-listened, gleaning small chunks of his insecure raging. "I'll prove them wrong," he said as his van chugged up the steep hill. "I've whipped up a tool unlike anything else the hunting world has seen. Jessie *can't* ignore me after this, not even for Emily—"

"Hate to interrupt your rendition of a cuckold's wettest dream, but we're here."

Beuzzle yelped and slammed on the breaks. I lurched forward, my forehead slamming into the dash, stars suddenly swimming in my vision. After I recovered, and had punched Beuzzle in the arm, I looked out of the van's window and was blinded by lights. Specifically *red and blue* lights.

Cops.

Chapter 10

Full of Surprises

Police!?" Beuzzle squeaked.

"Relax."

"There are *police* involved, Graves!? Why didn't you say anything!? Oh, God. Oh, Lord." He started breathing hard and darting his eyes around, pupils made huge behind his square glasses. He seemed ready to speed the hell outta there.

"I said fucking relax, damn it. They're probably just here to scope out the mansion; Jennifer called the cops a few weeks ago and asked for help — before she asked the Union, I mean. They don't have anything to find in there."

Well, except the destroyed, blood-soaked bedroom and the underground Nazi laboratory. But Beuzzle didn't have to know about that yet.

As you can tell from Beuzzle's reaction, hunters and police don't get along. Think about it this way: You're a cop, what would *you* do if some idiot wandered onto your crime scene claiming that a ghost did the deed? You'd either A) call them a big dumb-dumb then kick their ass outta there, or B) let them work at the scene — pointing and laughing — until they actually proved you wrong, making *you* the big dumb-dumb. Either way, blood boils whenever the two professions interact.

I noticed something odd about the whirling lights: Rather than emanating from a single bar atop a police car like you'd usually see, they were coming from a small spinning bulb… magnetized to the top of a dinky Camry.

Aubrey.

"Now *that* ain't good," I whispered.

"What? What isn't good, Graves?"

"Nothing to worry about," I said. "An old acquaintance happens to be snooping around, but she ain't a cop anymore" *I don't think she is, at least.*

"I... Yeah, okay." Beuzzle looked a little calmer as he caught his breath.

Of course, I thought, *if she* does *stumble on something suspicious in that mansion — say, a giant pool of blood — I'd most likely be going to jail anyway, and Beuzzle would probably be my cell-mate.*

We climbed out of Beuzzle's van. He dug in the back of the vehicle and ripped a few dorky-looking thingamabobs, shoving them in a cute backpack. One of the electronics was a messy jumble of wires — the thing he'd been working on back at his "headquarters."

Beuzzle's mouth gaped when he saw the front of Jennifer's mansion. With the setting sun, the dozens of windows rebounded a ghostly red hue, like the bloodshot eyes of a starving predator.

"I'm, uh, not so sure about this, Graves..."

"What? Oh. That's alright, sweetie," I cooed at him. "Say, do you have Emily's phone number, perchance? I'll need to get a *real* man over here, stat."

He glared at me but recovered his pace, striding determinedly towards the mansion.

"Woah..." he said, his voice echoing through the spacious halls of the haunt. "This place is *crazy*!"

"You see why I needed your tools, then."

"Yeah. I mean, this mansion could house the entire

population of Hartsville! I knew Jennifer Nee was rich, but wow..." He spent a minute appreciating the scope, then cleared his throat and said, "So... where *is* Jennifer, anyway?"

"Wouldn't you like to know, you horny little toad. She's preoccupied. Jennifer hired me — by that I mean Josephi, I guess — to find whatever was moaning under her house. I took care of the spook, but he had a friend — a much *quieter* friend, obviously."

"Gotcha," Beuzzle said. "I can still hear the hum. So what was the first ghost like?"

"Dead."

"Okay, but what was his history with the mansion? Why was he anchored to it? Did he put up a fight?"

"Not really."

Beuzzle narrowed his eyes at me. I stared flatly back. Man meets boulder, boulder won't budge, man walks around boulder. A tale as old as time.

"Alright, well, about where did you find the first ghost?" he asked.

"You think that maybe his friend would be close to where he was haunting?"

"No. I just need somewhere to start. This place is so huge that I wouldn't know bathroom from bedroom."

"Ah," I said. "Kitchen. That-a way."

Beuzzle frowned when he saw the mounds of coke stark against the black marble, but looked away and walked to where I'd destroyed the island. He gestured at the person-sized hole in the floor and raised an eyebrow at me. "I'm guessing this is about where it went down."

I didn't reply.

"Right," he sighed. "This is as good a place as any, I suppose."

He sat on the tile, crisscross, in front of the hole. I leaned against the wall and watched as Beuzzle brought out the little box he'd been working on earlier, with the bundled multicolored wire squished inside it. Squinting in focus, he looked sharply at his fingers. With a fiery flash, a bright spark came from his index finger and his thumb, leaving them coated in blue mist. Small wispy flames emanated from his fingertips like translucent turquoise mist.

He held the box in his lap and used his other hand to bring two of the wires together, squeezing the space between them with his glowing fingers. They sizzled and sparked, smoke hissing in a small stream as they were welded together. A bead of sweat fell down Beuzzle's cheek, which he wiped away with his free hand as he took the box off his lap. The wires fit nicely into it as Beuzzle pushed the two sides of the box together with a *snap*.

He stood and turned the device around in his hands, smiling. There wasn't much to it — no antennae at the top, no knobs on the front, no speaker. Though, there was a little button on its side, almost perfectly level with the center of the glass globe that protruded from the front plate like the screen of a CRT television.

"It's... *perfect*," the chubby medium whispered.

"Yeah, it's abso-fucking-lutely amazing. Now, how does it help us find the spook?"

"It doesn't," he replied, still marveling at his handiwork.

I resisted the urge to smack the stupid box right out of his hands and shove him into a gym locker, then asked, "So what the hell is it?"

"All in due time, my good man." He snickered wickedly, like a chunky Frankenstein.

"Beuzzle," I said warningly.

He finally snapped out of his technologically-fueled horniness. Standing and smiling at me apologetically,

Beuzzle dug into his backpack and whipped out a small metal ball, as shiny as chrome. It was around the size of an apple. "*This* will track down the ghost. It doesn't work much in the way of communication, but it'll at least point us in the right direction."

"Oh... you can't just talk to the spook from here?"

"Probably not. I have to be in the same room. Or at least *near* it."

Damn. I was kinda hoping that Beuzzle would've been able to pull the same trick he had at Mallery's, talking and communicating with the ghost without moving. I had a crazy feeling that the spook was waiting somewhere down in the giant Nazi laboratory/prison filled with human remains. The fewer people knew about *that* place the better, so I was banking that Beuzzle could use his satellite to confer with the ghost and draw it out of hiding... or something. I guess I hadn't really thought it through all that much.

Beuzzle squeezed the metallic ball in his hand. When he let go, the ball remained levitating where he'd been holding it. It didn't bob or shift, it simply *was*, like an invisible hand was still holding it firmly in place. Radiant blue prints were left wherever his fingers had pressed. He snapped two glowing fingers, the snap echoing through the kitchen as if he'd hit a piece of metal with a stick, and the ball levitated toward the other end of the kitchen. We followed.

Admittedly, I was impressed. Each member of the Union *has* to have a certain set of supernatural abilities, which usually restricts them to an inherent role within the hunting scene; I'm the sole exception to these rules. Mediums have the most limited set — that's why Josephi stayed in the Union despite not having any actual abilities — yet Beuzzle was doing some things I'd never seen with his comparatively minuscule powers.

Not to blow him too rigorously or anything, but it seemed I'd been a little too hard on the kid. I guess he had a lot to prove by tagging along here.

The ball had, surprisingly, not gone down the Nazi hole. Instead, it left through the side of the kitchen, moving back into the foyer. We followed it until it went down the same hallway that I'd dragged Beefboy through, then it stopped at the where that trapdoor was — right at the base of one of the towers. I expected the ball to start banging on the trapdoor, but it actually went *upwards*. We mounted the steps after it.

As I climbed, a thought occurred to me.

"Beuzzle."

"Y-yeah?" he asked, out of breath.

"Just so you're ready, this spook is a little... aggressive. He's probably more dangerous than anything you've faced before."

"I'm ready," he replied quickly.

"Now don't puss out on me— what did you say?"

"I said I'm ready."

"Huh," I grunted. "Alright then."

Eventually, the ball stopped. It levitated over the stairs, which crawled upwards with no end in sight. I thought it was broken or something, but after a second, it bounced gently against the wall to our left. Looking closely, I noticed a nearly invisible seam outlining what was clearly a door. I pushed against it and tried to dig my hands into its seam, but it wouldn't budge. Inspecting the wall around the door, I eventually noticed one brick with *slightly* less dense cement encasing it; little holes dotted the cement's texture. Frowning speculatively, I pushed the brick.

It moved about an inch, thumping against something hard behind it — metal, I thought. The door moved, brick grinding against brick, and slowly swung outwards. Behind it was only black. My flashlight revealed more brick, each bulging rectangle kept clean and straight inside this hidden passage. Beuzzle made a sick sound behind me. Honestly, I wasn't feeling great about the situation either.

The ball moved through the doorway and into the darkness beyond.

I felt the familiar sense of crossing the threshold into an age-old haunt — one supernaturally occupied for dozens of years. The death hum roared, a gurgling in this stone golem's hollow stomach. I kept my back straight and head calm, but Beuzzle panicked behind me. Well, if he wanted to prove that he had what it takes to be hunter, there was no better way than sneaking through a hidden passageway inside a Nazi's haunted mansion — that's textbook.

"M-man," Beuzzle mumbled, breaking the looming hum. "What *is* this place, Graves?"

"Beats me," I replied. "But I don't think anyone has set foot in here since..." Just then, I noticed hardly distinguishable footprints in the dust. Beefman's.

"F-footprints?" Gus whispered. "How could a ghost leave *footprints*?"

"He's not your average spook. As I said, this'll be more dangerous than anything you've ever seen." I thought for a moment, then said, "If you want to turn back, Beuzzle, I wouldn't blame you. You've done your job."

"The sphere would stop leading if I left," he said reluctantly.

I didn't reply, but the implication was there: Beuzzle *couldn't* leave. I needed to finish this.

After what felt like miles of walking through dust and shadows, surrounded by the ominously constant hum, we entered a large circular chamber. The ball provided some dim light, as did the flashlights on my shoulders, but the room was mostly lit by an opening in the ceiling, high, *high* above us. From what I could tell, the roof was actually sloping inwards. It led to a point at its tip, where the opening was. I even caught a few of the same symbols I'd seen in the lower laboratories carved and painted into the stone wall, still too faded to make out fully.

"This must be the other tower," Beuzzle deduced. "We were moving *inside* of the wall."

"I'd guess this is the only entrance."

The walls were lined with bookshelves. Lab equipment was littered all around: metallic tables, vats and beakers, crumpled and shredded papers. In the chamber's center, a chair sat on top of a metal pole. It looked like something you'd see in a dentist's office, except for the braces drilled into its armrests and the glass helmet attached to its headrest. The helmet had a little spike of metal coming from the top, like an antenna. A lever protruded from the brick next to the chair, as well as a small screen with the 1940s version of a keyboard attached to it.

All in all, I got a distinctly Frankensteinian vibe from the place. Which I'd say is pretty much never good.

Walking further into the chamber, I heard a thumping noise coming from far above us. The ball floated upwards quickly and, when it got high enough, I could make out a thick wooden platform built into the circular wall. A rectangular hole was carved into the center of the platform, sunlight spilling through it. There was a metal ladder to the far right, which travelled downwards and rooted on ground-level.

Me and Beuzzle shared a look, then I started towards the ladder.

Whimpers of fear and weary growls came into my hearing the further I climbed. A source of light — different than both the hole in the ceiling and Beuzzle's ball — streamed through the platform's opening, this one more of a bleach white.

I'd recognize Baby's glow anywhere.

We reached the top of the ladder. A smaller, person-sized opening was right above me, growls and whimpers leaking through it. I looked down at Beuzzle and mouthed, *stay here.* He nodded shakily.

This was gonna be a fuckin' challenge. Beefman was not only incredibly strong and fast, he seemingly healed *fatal* wounds. My sword should have Severed him the second she drove through his guts, but it wasn't working. Plus, he would likely be wielding Baby. In his hands, she wouldn't especially strong — but still, she's a fuckin' *greatsword.* Enough said.

My thoughts gathered, head cleared, and nerves calmed, I pulled myself quickly onto the platform. And saw something I couldn't have possibly imagined.

Jennifer was not dead. She wasn't gored, or beheaded, or bisected — far, *far* from it. Jennifer was alive and well — panicking, clearly, but breathing. As for Beefman, he looked about as ferocious as before, except for the rings of blood that encircled his limbs; one arm had *ten* thin lines of crimson. Lumps of meat decorated the floor, some still leaking blood, creating pools. Others even twitched, still fresh. Beefman's breath was labored as he stared at Jennifer from across the room. Surprisingly, he wasn't holding Baby.

Jennifer was.

The Blade's light was dimmed, ounces of blood coating her steel. Thick dollops of skin and muscle fell from her, *splatting* on the floor sickeningly. Jennifer herself was covered in red, hair and bare pale skin frosted like a cake. Even more surprising than the blood, though, was the glow that surrounded her. It was the same shade as Baby's.

Her eyes were wide, distant, and her breaths came shallow

and rapid. She was holding Baby in front of her — an impressive feat considering the Blade's weight — warding off Beefman, who had begun prowling and studying her like a wolf would his prey. That's when it all clicked.

Jennifer had spent the hours since I was thrown out that window repeatedly severing Beefman's limbs — arm after arm, leg after leg — to keep him at bay. And it had fucking worked.

Severing a limb with a greatsword is a pretty difficult accomplishment, even for someone as sturdy as me. I didn't fool myself into thinking that Jennifer — a frail, twenty-year-old woman presumably already exhausted from countless hours of love-making — was able to muster up the strength to do so repeatedly for over a dozen hours, so Baby must have given Jennifer herself some added strength and stamina. And it looked like the Blade would have the same effect on Beefman's flesh she does on a spook's spectral mass. That was good to fuckin' know.

Jennifer let out a squeak of fear when she noticed me standing there. She shivered with terror and tiredness, dawning a look of exasperated relief. Almost instantly, she passed out from exhaustion. Baby pulsed tiredly in her limp grip.

"Girl, you're full of surprises," I whispered. I'd *never* seen an average mortal wield her before. Hell, I didn't even think it was *possible* — but I guess Baby had made an exception for little ol' Jenny.

Beefman perked up when he noticed that Jennifer was unconscious, a hungry grin spreading across his bloodied face. I reached down and gently pulled Baby out of Jennifer's loosened grip, then faced the naked ogre.

"How about you try me, instead?" I said, keeping myself steady. "I promise I don't bite. Me, you, and Baby — call it a threesome."

His leer melted into a grimace of rage. He roared — a noise like a dog's thundering bark mixed with a gorilla's primal yell — then came bounding towards me. I readied myself, spreading my legs, bending my knees slightly, and leveling Baby next to my head. I positioned the flat of her blade next to my face and held her grip tightly. She was steady in my hands; my breath came softly. I was a snake coiled and ready to strike.

Beefman leaped from the wooden platform, flying higher than any regular human would be able to. Waiting until the last moment, right when his sneering mug was inches away from mine, I spun out of the way. Without looking, just feeling and instinctually judging placement and movement, I swung Baby downwards in a perfect arch. Just as I thought, she passed through Beefman's waist like a spoon through pudding.

His two halves fell to the ground with a pair of dusty *thuds*. Purple and red innards spilled out like worms from freshly dampened earth. I whipped Baby around, cleaning most of the viscera off of her and aiming back at Beefman. He struggled and writhed in his own blood, but otherwise didn't seem like he was getting back up, thank God. Baby vibrated and hummed with that final slaughter, relishing in the bloodbath that'd doused her shining steel.

I worried about how I'd explain away Beefman's death, but, seeing as he had been continuously de-limbed for sixteen hours and still came out of it unscathed, I saw no other way. The cops could make all the fuss they want, but Jennifer would be there to back me up. I'm not crazy about killing normies but—

"Oh, no fucking way."

Two milky white lumps grew where Beefman's waist

ended. Mist *coated* his midsection, so thick it was almost fog. The lumps enlarged as layers of red muscle swirled around them. Quickly, as I went running towards Beefman to finish the job before he could recuperate, the muscle grew into the obvious shape of thighs, then calves, then feet.

Beefman leaped off the ground using just his arms. He spun in the air, somehow majestically, and *punched* me in the chest. I felt something *crack* as he did, and I flew backwards, crashing and skidding on the floor like a ragdoll.

Gasping for breath, I tried to turn and lay on my back, but it was just too painful. Beefman's still raw feet slapped against the wood as he shambled towards me, presumably to crush my head like a tin can. My breath wouldn't come naturally. I was getting lightheaded from lack of oxygen and an abundance of searing, throbbing pain. Beefman's steps continued thudding, like my heart beating its last beats. He reached me slowly but surely; he heaved ragged, wet breaths as he stood over me. Beefman took his time contemplating how to kill me — *Rip off his limbs? Scalp him with my bare nails? Twist his head until the sinew and skin tear like cloth?*

But before he could do any of those things, something echoed behind him. A nasally voice rang out, sounding faded and ghostly through my exhaustion.

"H-hey! You, ah, big idiot! Mess with someone your own s-size!"

I could practically *hear* Beefman crack a ravenous grin as he left me and strutted towards Beuzzle.

Beuzzle, I thought, too pained to shout, *you fucking moron.*

"Yeah, that's r-right!" he said, voice shaking in terror. "Come and get me!"

Beefman's now skin-covered feet thudded on the wood as he broke into a full sprint. Pants pushed from his jowls as if he were a starving dog with a dripping steak just out of reach.

Grunting in anguish, I rolled onto my back. Beefman hadn't made it *too* far. There was still some hope.

I reached back, my chest screaming and begging for me to stop, and drew my shotgun. Shells flew from their containers and into the shotty when I cracked open the chamber. I aimed down the sights towards Beefman's back. The weapon's kick made me *scream;* I almost passed out from the sheer agony of it. Beefman turned at both the thunderous roar of the shotgun and my shriek, just in time to see the two clean shells *explode* a few feet in front of him. Shrapnel spread out in a rain of metal. Beefman howled as it pierced and shredded skin and flesh like paper. He recoiled from the shock and pain, but blue mist was already rushing to heal his wounds.

That was it. That was all I could do.

But it wasn't all *Gus* could do.

Shakily, Gus whipped out his little box, his pride and joy. I saw him press the button on its side. The machine whirred as it sprung to life. A sucking sound, like that of an extra powerful vacuum, came from within it. Beefman's mist was almost done with its arduous work...

It started stripping away, sucked into Gus' device like water down a drain.

Beefman growled and resumed his bounding, blue mist still streaming from him and into the box. Gus screamed shrilly, but the guy still held out his device towards Beefman, shaking but prepared.

The monster's footsteps skidded to a halt when he was just a few steps away from Gus. He fell to his knees, breath becoming faint. The blue mist dwindled; less and less was coming off of Beefman's dripping wounds. With one final gasp, the last of the mist was sucked out of him. He fell, face forward, onto the ground with a crash. The device's glow pierced the darkness like a miniature blue sun, illuminating

Gus' stupid grin. He laughed madly with relief and kissed the glowing glass bulb that jutted out of his tool.

"You stupid son of a bitch," I groaned, pain joining the words — then I chuckled, which hurt even worse. "You actually fucking did it."

Chapter 11

Canned

Climbing down that ladder *would* have been painful, but with Jennifer thrown over one shoulder it was downright excruciating. Even tougher when I was trying to ignore her soft breasts pressed against my shoulder, tips made erect and palpable even through Gus' sweater vest.

Gus made it to the heavenly floor first, then whispered encouragement as if he'd actually be able to catch me if I fell. I leaped the last few rungs, too tired to climb the rest of the way, and landed with a shockwave of writhing pain. Gus sighed in relief, as I would have if my teeth weren't clenched nearly hard enough to crack.

My nerves were much less sharp as we stomped back through the dark hidden corridor. Gus held his little doohickey, and I had Baby slung over my other shoulder, both lighting the way.

"What the hell is that thing, anyway?" I said, wincing with every step.

He stared at the device like it was his first-born child. "Haven't thought of a name yet."

"Okay, then what did it do to that spook? Is he in the Other Side yet?"

"What? Oh. No." Gus looked sort of mesmerized as he said that, still looking at the device and its glowing glass protrusion. Glancing closer, it really *did* resemble a CRT's screen.

"Gus. Where is the ghost," I demanded.

He smiled wickedly at me, then nodded his head towards the white-blue glow.

"No shit... you mean you *captured* the fucker? Like, not in a ring of fucking salt or a pentagram or some shit, but a legit *cage?*"

"That's about the size of it."

"Damn... So what now, hot stuff? What do we do with the spook?"

"I, ah, haven't really figured that part out yet — how to get rid of him, at least. Pressing this button again will let the ghost out, but I'll need someone here to do the... dirty work."

"Yeah. I'll take care of him," I said, shifting Baby on my shoulder and grinding my aching bones together. "Just let me get some fucking orange juice or something. I think that douchebag cracked a rib."

We made it to a dead end, what I figured was the hidden door that had opened from the spiral staircase. Gus pushed his shoulder against it and it clicked, then swung inwards. We stepped out, different men than when we'd entered.

I jumped as Gus gasped at something to our right — specifically a thing with tight pants hugging a pair of hips that could kill.

Aubrey had her ear against the wall, but leaped back at Gus' sharp inhale.

"Graves? What the fuck? *When* the fuck—"

"*Who* the fuck? *Why* the fuck?" I said. "These quandaries haunt my very dreams, Aubrey."

She quickly contained her shock and crossed her arms, glaring at me and ignoring Gus. "I *knew* this wasn't as cut and dry as you were making it out to be," Aubrey said. "I just had to come see for myself."

"Uh-huh," I said. "You're ever the sleuth, Aubrey. I truly can't believe you found this spooky hidden door that we just opened in front of you."

She grimaced, full lips down turning in an angry frown. "I'm gonna have your ass for this, Graves."

"Oh, is my ass your main motivator? Should have known." I flashed her a smile. "Do you have any *proof* that might earn you said ass? Or are you just spouting nonsense out of yours?"

"Oh, I don't know." She grinned maliciously. "How about your blood-soaked clothes? Or maybe the fact that you just stepped out of a hidden passageway previously undocumented in this mansion's blueprints? Or, hey, how about the fucking unconscious *pop idol* you're carrying?"

Okay, I'll admit I wasn't in peak thinking condition. My injuries and the ungodly energy I'd exerted were weighing on me. I needed a meal. Stat.

Aubrey chuckled. "You are so fucked—"

"Police lights," Gus said, nervously and suddenly. Aubrey turned and looked him up and down, like she'd just noticed he was there.

"Excuse me?" she said in a tone that would unnerve anyone.

"You had a police light attached to your Camry."

"Your point?"

Then it dawned me. *Gus, you wonderful, chubby angel.*

"You're out of commission, Aubrey," I said, gasping through the pain yet still grinning at her. She made no comment, emotion melting from her face. "I can't help but think the commissioner would be nonplussed with you *impersonating an officer*." I tsked. "Bad, bad girl."

"What makes you think I'm out of a job?" she asked, voice solid.

"Well, for starters, I'm not sure Investigations would spend their very limited manpower — or womanpower — investigating a case and location that have already been thoroughly searched by another branch of the police." I waited for a reaction, but she remained plain-faced. "And — as much as it hurts my tender little heart to admit this — I think you'd do *everything* in your power to avoid working near me. Yet here you are, desperate and alone."

We stared at each other for a second. Gus waited awkwardly next to us, glowing box still in hand.

"So, what now," Aubrey said, finally.

"I've gotta deal for you," I said. "You don't tell anyone what you saw here, and *I* won't tell your boss — er, *ex*-boss — that you were investigating without a badge."

She shook her head. "Not good enough, Graves. I *need* this. I'd gladly take the risk of the commissioner firing me permanently if it meant just the *chance* of getting back in his good graces."

Shit. She *was* desperate. "Okay, how about this: I won't tell your boss, you don't tell anyone we're involved, *and* you get to take over the investigation." I raised an eyebrow at her, waiting for a reaction.

She contemplated, then said, "Alright, that could work—"

"*But*," I cut in, "you can only take over *after* I've dealt with the supernatural side of things."

If the police investigated and discovered — or were even *possessed* by — a ghost, the Union would pull out ASAP. I just needed to take care of Gus' spook; everything after that wasn't of any concern — not after I got paid, at least.

Aubrey laughed. "You *still* believe in this shit, Graves? Didn't your mommy tell you the Boogeyman doesn't exist? What's next? Do you still leave cookies out for Santa too?"

"Aubrey, look around you. You're in a decrepit Nazi's

mansion, riddled with hidden passageways and sketchy laboratories straight out of a sci-fi flick — did I forget to mention those? Anyway, now you've stumbled upon me and my cohort lugging an unconscious, blood-soaked, half naked singer and an unheard-of device filled with glowing blue mist. Oh, and I'm carrying a fucking *magical sword*, Aubrey."

"I'm sure all of those things have real-world explanations," she said.

"Such as?"

She looked at me, my expression genuinely open to any suggestion she might have, then faced the ground, nibbling on her lip and twisting the corner of her collar with two fingers. "Fine. I don't know what the fuck is going on here, but I still hold that it has nothing to do with anything *paranormal*."

"Aubrey, come the fuck—"

"But," she said, "I'll give you your time. Just let me know when I can step in and get any evidence I need to get a real investigation going."

"Alrighty, then. It's a deal," I agreed, winking at her. Now that all of this negotiating was dealt with, I noticed the searing heat still flaring in my chest and Jennifer's weight on my shoulder. "I hate to cut our wonderful conversation short, but I really need to go fucking sit down or something."

I reached back and sheathed Baby, grinding my teeth through the pain. Aubrey walked closer and put her arms out, bottoms up. I got the hint, slinging Jennifer off my shoulder and placing her in Aubrey's arms, wedding style. "Christ," I groaned and dug my knuckles into the small of my back. "Thank you." She nodded silently and we descended the stairs, Gus behind us, studying his contraption.

"What's her deal?" Aubrey asked.

"Yeah, Graves?" Gus said.

"She'll be okay. I took care of it."

She nodded again, surprisingly trusting. Well, even if she didn't believe in the Other Side and all that came with it, she'd still seen me accomplish some pretty impressive feats — *especially* considering that she thought my physical prowess was entirely rooted in the mundane.

"Graves," she piped in.

"What's up?"

Aubrey looked at her shoes as they fell on the stairs, deep in thought. There was a sense of vulnerability to her body language, more than I'd ever seen. I got the feeling she needed some kinship, like she'd been lonely for a while now.

"If you fuck me on this," she said, matter-of-factly, "I'll fucking end you."

"Uh... understood."

We wrapped Jennifer in some blankets that Aubrey had gotten from her car and lay her on the floor in the kitchen, rather than on her blood-soaked bed.

"What are we going to do with her?" Gus asked.

Me and Aubrey shared a look.

"I don't think we can call 911," I said. "If the same guys are driving the ambulance, they'll start associating my face with drug-infused unconscious people. Which means the cops would probably start catching a whiff of shit."

Gus nodded solemnly then looked at Aubrey.

"I'm not even supposed to be here, kid," she said. "I was only tagging along the first time because I knew the ambulance driver. He wouldn't let it slide if he saw me hanging around here again."

"Neither of us can drop her off at the hospital, either," I said. "Everyone knows exactly where Jennifer Nee lives, so it'd be just as incriminating as them actually *coming* to the mansion and finding us here."

Gus took the hint. "It's not gonna look great having a naked pop idol passed out in my van." He swallowed, looking down at the calmly snoozing musician. "But I guess we've got no choice."

"Attaboy." I slapped him on the shoulder.

"We're not done here, Graves. We still have to help the girls. And don't forget about the guy I sucked into my little box."

"Don't say that in the wrong part of town," I said. Neither of them laughed. They must have not heard me. "You'll have to leave the spook here. How contained do you think he is in that thing?"

"Oh, he won't be going anywhere." Gus fished out the box and shook it. The blue mist didn't move at all, like water when you spin a glass. He tossed the box at me. I caught it with a sigh of effort, then placed it on the kitchen's counter.

Crickets chirped around us as we carried Jennifer outside and into the crisp night air. Autumn had fully taken over, sapping each day's light slowly but steadily. The stars were pinpricks in the heavens, like cigarette burns in a deep-blue tapestry. Wisps of clouds had started inches across the night's face, dark and foreboding.

I placed Jennifer in the passenger's seat of Gus' van and buckled her in. She hardly shifted, her breaths shallow from sheer exhaustion. Gus climbed in and started the vehicle, puffs of smoke burping out of its tailpipe.

"What say we meet tomorrow morning and finish the job," I said.

"Really?" Gus replied. "You wouldn't rather take it on tonight?"

I glared at him and gestured towards my most likely broken ribs, grunting in pain just from that slight movement.

"Ah," he said. "Alright, then."

We agreed to meet up the next morning at the bottom of Jennifer's hill, then he drove off. Leaving me and Aubrey alone.

"So..." I said, after a silence, "how about a ride?

She pivoted on her heel and started walking towards her Camry without another word.

"Wait!" She turned around, halfway inside her car, and gave me a flat look. "Please?"

Aubrey kept up her glare, then rolled her eyes and gestured towards the passenger seat. "Aubrey, you're a saint! My princess in shining, bedazzled armor! My—"

"Don't fucking push it, Graves."

I smiled at her and said, "How about some dinner? On me?"

After another hour of flat staring, she grunted affirmatively.

"Gee," Aubrey said, poking at her Grand Slamwich, "you sure know how to treat a lady."

"Y'know, I've always thought that." I scoffed, bits of eggs and bacon flying from my mouth. "Guess some women just can't appreciate chivalry." I leaned over and slurped the last of my drink through a bendy straw, making sure to snatch all of the dregs from the bottom. A waitress strolled over, clothes bright red and yellow, a symbol of Denny's pride.

"Would you like a refill, sweetie?" Her eyes were tired and emotionless.

"Yes, please." She picked up my empty glass and walked back into the kitchen. I polished off my hash browns and moved on to my mountain of pancakes, thinly spreading butter and dumping syrup on them.

"You're a child," Aubrey said.

"Hey," I managed through a mouthful of delicious, soft sweetness, "a man needs to refuel after a day's hard work." The waitress came back and placed a glass in front of me, filled with a frothy sweet liquid. I winked at her and continued my feast.

"With chocolate milk," Aubrey said. I shrugged and emptied the glass. My body was already repairing my cracked ribs, chocolate milk and shitty eggs and shittier pancakes literally keeping me alive. The jumpsuit would cover any of the blue mist hard at work healing and revitalizing me.

She pressed her plump lips to the rim of her mug and nursed some of her black coffee, staring out the window and towards the town, made black and blue by night. 1960s music thrummed softly through the speakers in the diner, accented by a few booths' worth of idle chit chat and utensils scraping plates.

"So," I said, now halfway through my cakes, "booted from the force, huh?"

Aubrey gave me a sideways look with eyes like emeralds. I shrugged, letting her know I didn't care all that much, but that she could still vent if she wanted to.

"Yeah," she sighed. "Over basically fucking nothing"

"Mm-hmm," I said, chewing loudly. "Go on."

"Little brat downtown, seventeen years old — you know how it is there."

"Yup."

"He'd been doing meth for years; we all knew it, but what was one more doped-up kid, right? The commissioner wouldn't let me do shit about it." She placed the mug back on the table, frowning — from the bitter coffee or her thoughts, I didn't know. "Until we found out he wasn't *from* downtown. He's a rich boy. Mommy's some bigwig at a pharmaceutical company. That's when the boss gets serious, that's when he sends us to scare him straight — the parents came a-calling."

I took a sip of chocolate milk, careful to keep it from slurping against the glass.

"Well, we found the kid," Aubrey continued. "But he wasn't alone. He had his sister there with him — his thirteen-year-old sister. We kicked them in the ass and sent them home, even kept the boy in lockup overnight. The girl was clean, passed every drug test." She grimaced, eyes lost in the tar-black drink in front of her.

"What then? Why'd you get canned?"

"Another call, a few nights later. The parents say their girl's sick and they don't know what to do about it. If it's an overdose, how can they take her to the hospital? They have an image to retain, after fucking all."

I swallowed the last bite of my cakes, hardly chewed.

"We show up just in time for the girl to choke on her own spit, suffocate, and die." Aubrey's teeth showed. "*Fucking thirteen* goddamnit. It was her piece-of-shit brother who gave it to her. I think he wanted to see what happened, that dumb fucker." Her temples pulsed with the flexing of her jaw. I looked into her grass-green eyes, but she broke the stare.

"Anyway, I beat the fuck outta the kid. Tubman says I'm unfit to serve, that I have to get my anger under control. But I know he was just trying to appease those shithead parents — those fucking failures. I should've fucking..." She trailed off, blinking aggressively. Moonlight reflected off the smallest bit of moisture underneath each eye.

"And you think Tubman'll give you your job back if you crack a big case?" I asked, slurping down the last bit of milk.

"I think I'd try anything at this point. Even if I have to work for those corrupt fucks... I'd be nothing if I weren't a cop." Aubrey locked eyes with me.

“I’m sure you’d be plenty.” I winked at her and smiled widely. She rolled her eyes and slumped back, but her shoulders were less rigid than before. Finally, she picked up half of the Slamwich and started eating.

“See? Aren’t I the best date?” I said, reaching across the booth and grabbing the other half.

Chapter 12

Days Long Passed

I wasn't surprised when Agatha showed up in my bedroom that night, but the lack of spontaneity didn't make it any less fucking annoying.

"What do you want," I said, swinging my legs over the edge of my cot and rubbing the thick sleep from my eyes.

"It's not what *I* want—"

"It's what *he* wants," I finished. "You bozos really need some new shtick."

She ignored me. "It is the dawn of your final day, Bastard. You have 24 hours to deliver me an adequate host. After you fail, you die."

"Okay? What, you think I forgot?"

At that, she frowned, ink-black eyes intent on mine. "Ah... so petulant, like a spoiled child prevented his toy. Is such an attitude befitting a man like you?"

"Why not? Who do I have to impress? *You?"*

The demi-goddess floated a few feet closer. "Hmm, maybe in days long passed, yes; our match may have brought each of us power both physical and political. As well as certain... other pleasantries." Her small tongue poked out and lightly touched one plump pink lip.

"Yeah, I'd rather get fucked by a lamp-post."

Agatha's laugh was like crystals tinkling into a clear pool. "I promise you the feeling is mutual, Bastard."

"Don't fucking call me that," I growled.

"Oh? You still deny your past? Regardless, now you have less worth to me than the wriggling worm between your legs. You should have not left us, *Bastard*; your fate was sealed the moment you fled the Bowels."

I relaxed a little. "First off, it's more a python, less a worm. Second, every minute I spent in that shithole would've brought me one step closer to slaughtering the lot of you — you're hardly worth the mess." I scratched my belly, smiling at her annoyingly.

"Slaughter *us*?" she scoffed. "We *praised* you, Bastard. A Warrior of God! Now *that* is a conquest. Every demon in the Other Side and its Bowels were like to kneel before you, yet you shunned us — fled with your shame tucked firmly behind you."

"Not before giving the Reaper a small love tap, if I recall."

"Oh yes. You struck a cheap blow, Bastard, then you fled all the same. I will admit I was impressed when I heard of Death's injuries; even if he is not at his full power, that was not an easy feat."

"Thank you," I said. "And he's powerful enough."

She sneered, pretty lips puckering. Agatha was steadily moving forward. Her radiant brilliance blasted my shadow behind me, making each patch of darkness in the small bedroom black as rot. "The Reaper is weakening. None know why, but it is truth." Her teeth were gleaming pearls. "I plan to be there, to pick up the pieces." It was hardly a whisper. "Your Blade will all but secure that position."

I scowled. "You fucking wish. Baby is as much mine as the moment she was given to me, and that won't change in a day. You can say your prayers, Agatha, but that won't change shit. Expect your host with a swirl of whipped cream and a cherry on top."

"Your denial has reached levels unheard of, Bastard. I suppose I would expect nothing less; how could you possibly live with yourself, after what you've done? You were always weak that way — so loyal to your more humanly impulses. If I were in your place, a kill like that would give me such elation that even *you* couldn't dampen my spirits." She licked her lips again. "And let's not forget the prize: Chronalius, delivered to you on a silver plate." Agatha leaned forward, bringing her beautiful, shapely face just inches from mine, giving me a peek at her buoyant cleavage. She smelled like lavender. I frowned.

"*Gifted to you*," she mocked. "Ha! The Blade of Balance was *stolen*, Bastard, from its original owner. In an act more *wicked* than any I've ever witnessed, the Warrior of God Ursula was struck down by a blow most unsuspected. Killed by her own—"

"Agatha," I snarled. "Do us both a fucking favor and shut your otherworldly trap."

Her laughter tinkled again. "Oh, spare me the bravado, Graves. Just because your life is so comparatively short does not mean you must rush to face death. Your Blade is hardly as powerful as it once was, while it was in Ursula's hands. Even with Chronalius, I would slice you into dripping red ribbons."

"I know I've got a lot riding here," I said, bringing my own face even closer. "I know that the Reaper doesn't think much of me right now, and that he'd kill me as swiftly as anyone else. But if you bring her up again, my fucks will dissipate like sugar in water." My growl was rumbling and bestial. "I'll save you the 24 hours and kill you where you stand, bitch. Is that clear?"

Sniffing with contempt, Agatha broke away from my glare and turned to leave. I caught a sleeve of her flowing gown.

"Answer me, or I'll cut you in half right fucking now. I'll sop up your blood with a sponge and wring it into my waiting mouth. Millenia of life, snuffed out easier than a candle's fucking flame. You'll regret ever—"

"Enough," Agatha said. "In 24 hours, all answers will be had. Your innocence will be disproven once and for all, and Chronalius will be mine." The radiance enraptured her, leaving only Agatha's dark eyes, like pools of obsidian. "Midnight tonight, Bastard of Death," she said. Then she was gone.

Thankfully, I managed to wake up early. Angry clouds almost masked the rising sun, so the landscape was draped in stubborn shadow — a night that wasn't ready to give up its throne. Birds nervously tittered their greetings to the morning, knowing that the hands of time had ticked one notch closer to the ever-looming winter.

Throwing my covers off me was to break out of a cocoon of warmth. Even Hans seemed to pout at the sudden upheaval, but I shrugged at him and said, "This could be my last day in this realm, pal. I'd like to savor every moment."

Speaking of savoring, I still had *two* eggs left in the fridge. Halleluyah. I hardboiled 'em, washed them down with some stale beer, then started prepping.

It seemed my ribs had healed overnight, thank the Lord, and I walked with a little extra skip in my step. I'd used a good portion of my shells the previous day, so I slotted a few new bullets into their holsters. I gave Baby a firm polishing, kissed the flat of her blade, then sheathed her gently, apologetic for leaving her for so long the previous day.

Oh, and I took a cold shower. I smelled like death, probably because of the previous day's multiple sweaty brawls and showers of blood.

Hans rubbed my leg as I was about to leave. He seemed to be sorrowfully saying goodbye... like he knew this might be the last chance he'd have to do so. I picked him up and gave him a big squeeze — he purred louder than a sports car going 150 — and left him to his slop, walking out into the colder cold.

Stretching and bending my joints, I was feeling pretty spry. I decided to forego the taxi, seeing as there's pretty much only one driver in all of Hartsville, and I doubted he wanted to return to that haunt so soon.

'Sides. I had a stop to make.

For some reason, I didn't expect Josephi to answer his phone, so I made my way into downtown with a song in my heart and a death on my mind. Members of the Union have to list their addresses and contact information on their exclusive website, so I hunted down the conman's abode in record time. Naturally, he lived far away from his office, in one of the nicer flats in town, with a sleek, flat roof and clean walls.

I debated on whether to actually knock. I figured Josephi deserved to have his door kicked down for playing with me again... though I was still unsure what he'd actually done or why. Better to play it cordial at first; my knuckles rapped loudly on the door. Scrambling came from the other side, like someone had been shocked awake and was now running to get everything in order.

"Who is it?" came Josephi's charming voice — the one he used to woo grieving customers or while fooling hopeful widows on *Answers From the Other Side*. I have no idea why some demi-god hadn't come up to rip Josephi's head off yet.

"It's the fist-up-your-asshole that you ordered, sir," I said pleasantly. "You'd best hurry. It's gettin' cold."

"Ah, shit," I heard him mumble. After a minute or two of

hasty scrambling, several locks unlatched and the door cracked open. "Ess naht a great time right now, Graves."

"Oh, I'm sorry. When would be better? Before or after you bent me over and had your way with my no-no zone?"

"I got no idea what you're talkin' about."

"Josephi, I ain't playing this game right now. Open the door or you'll be eating its splinters."

"Graves, I'm telling ya. Whatever you think is—"

"Five," I interrupted calmly.

"C'mon, man. Ain't we partners?"

"Four."

"What about duh Union!? Dey won't juss let you—"

"Fucking threeee," I sang.

He sighed. "Fine."

Josephi started to pull the door open slowly, so I pushed it with my shoulder to help him along. The inside of Josephi's flat was of an ilk with his office: gaudy, stylish, and well kept. Dozens of awards lined the walls and various surfaces — dressers, tables, windowsills. Despite how luxurious the place was, it was still a one-bedroom, one-bath, small kitchen kinda deal. In fact, I'm pretty sure my shack had more surface area. A large bed was pulled out from a couch, flush with the back wall. Josephi was in a red bathrobe cut just a hair too short.

"Y'know, I've seen just one dick too many recently," I said.

Josephi straightened his robe.

A pair of sultry giggles came from behind him. On the pullout bed, bundled up and looking warm in a few different ways, were the two brunette twins from the day before, thin blankets just barely covering their generous chests. I sighed internally. *Even this pencil-dick is getting laid.*

"Ladies. I'm sure your pah is smiling upon you from

above." That sapped pretty much any joviality from them; they sneered at me as if I were a skunk on the freeway.

"Y'know, Josephi," I said, ignoring them and draping an arm around his shoulder, "a lesser man might have lost his patience with you by now." I sat him at a small table in the corner of his flat. "A lesser man may have resorted to force. May have slipped up, let his anger get the best of him." I flashed my teeth. "Maybe they would have grabbed you by the neck and bashed your head against this fine glass table until it passed for an avant-garde art piece, and your face for a plate of apple sauce." He winced and whimpered quietly when I gripped his shoulders. "But I ain't that man. I can be *reasonable*, Josephi. Especially in the face of honesty." I strolled over and sat across from him, lacing my hands politely on the table. "So, is there anything you'd like to tell me?"

Josephi gulped and looked everywhere except for my eyes. "I... uh..." he stammered, hands gripping knees until his knuckles went white. "I'm sorry, Graves. I..." He shut his eyes so tight that his lashes nearly disappeared. "I still don't know what you're talkin' about."

"Really? Nothing?" I pursed my lips. "Not even about a certain deal with a certain medium?"

"No. Ess naht like that—" I slammed my fists onto the glass table, cracking its surface. Deafening silence ensued, which I was more than happy to leave empty. Josephi panicked, eyes darting around the room, trying to find some way to weasel his way out. Not this time. I'd rather beat his fucking—

Josephi suddenly stood up and ran quickly towards his nightstand on the other side of the pullout bed, vaulting over the very confused twins. He rummaged through the drawer in his nightstand and came out with a small notebook and a pencil. The chair squeaked as he plopped his bare ass back into it, then he started scribbling.

"What?" I growled. "You're writing me a check? You really think you can pay me off? I oughta break your—"

"I *think* I gotta solution fah *both* ya problems, Graves."

Both? I thought. "You mean the case at Jennifer's mansion?" He gave no sign. "What's my other problem, then? I'll be sittin' pretty after the Great Nazi Ghost Mystery is through with," I lied.

Josephi stopped writing abruptly and looked up at me. His pupils flicked quickly towards Baby's hilt, jutting out of her sheathe on my back. We locked eyes for a moment, then he continued writing.

No shit, I thought. *He found me a host? How the fuck is that possible? How the fuck did he even know that I needed one?* A whirlwind of possibilities whipped through my head, but one truth rang out in each: Josephi knew more about my situation than he should have.

Finally, he finished writing. He ripped out the piece of lined paper and handed it to me. It was an address. I raised an eyebrow questioningly, but he clenched his jaw. I knew that look; for whatever reason, Josephi wasn't allowed to speak on the matter. That unnerved me. He knew there was a *chance* that I'd beat his head in if he didn't give me answers, so whatever was holding his tongue must have been an even more pressing danger than *me*.

I had my suspicions, but you know what they say about assuming: It'll get you killed or whatever. I'd have to do my own investigating, so Josephi was safe for now.

Josephi stared at me. I narrowed my eyes at him, then left without another word.

First things first, I had to meet up with Gus and deal with the Detectors' little issue — plus the spook he'd caught in his little box the day before. I was sure both of those would go swimmingly.

As fucking if.

Chapter 13

Damsels

In a stroke of luck, Gus and I arrived at the base of the mansion's hill at almost the exact same time. He gave me a lift to the entrance, and we walked in and started planning.

"Our spook is still tucked nicely in your 'little box'?" I asked.

"He is," Gus replied, peering into the glass bulb. "The Specterencasing Cuboid essentially knocks them unconscious — at least, as much as a ghost *can* be knocked unconscious — and leaves them dormant and in their rawest spectral form: a sort of luminescent gas, as you can see."

"So you press the button on the side and the genie comes out of his bottle, yeah? Will he still be asleep or am I coming up against a full-force spook here?"

"Honestly, I'm not sure. The Specterencasing Cuboid is completely untested. Kind of a miracle that it even *worked* yesterday." There was a silence in which we both imagined what would've gone down if the thing *hadn't* worked. Gus shivered and said, "Anyway, I'm feeling optimistic considering it did what it was supposed to in the first place. Theoretically, the ghost should come out drowsy and ready for the Severing. If not..."

"I'll handle it," I said, drawing Baby.

"Yeah? You're not too injured?" Gus asked.

"Nah. Right as rain."

He narrowed his eyes at me, but shrugged and placed the Spectfuckining Whateverboid on the counter.

"Ready?"

"You betcha." I gave him a childish thumbs up.

Gus took a deep breath and pressed the button. The device instantly vibrated, its bottom rattling on the counter like change in a dryer. Mist leaked from its side and into the kitchen with as much force as steam from a tea kettle — except, instead of fading away, the mist lingered and coagulated. Eventually, the device slowed to a churning rumble, then it stopped, glass bulb empty. I thought that was it — that the spook was trapped in its gaseous state.

Then the mist squished and molded into body parts: arms, legs, hands, feet, a beefy torso. And a head.

And, I'm using *head* generously.

It was lumpy and malformed, like a basketball, only half-filled with air. It had no hair, but raw spots and dried blood dotted its scalp. The spook's nose was so wide and upturned that it looked more like a pig's snout. One ear was shaved to a point while the other had barely enough flesh to even be *called* an ear. An excess of skin had permanently grown on its cheeks and forehead, almost covering its beady, inhuman eyes. Its lips looked like deflated balloons, and its mouth was stuffed with teeth either rotten or sharp as a fox's fangs. The tongue was swollen; the spook had seemingly chewed the sides raw and even ripped some chunks of flesh clean off.

A metal plate was drilled into its temple. Just like a certain charred skull that I'd found in the secret Nazi laboratory.

The spook let out a gurgling cry, less primal than when it had been inside of Beefman, yet somehow even less human. It brought the same instinctual panic that hearing a rodent or pig squeal in agony did; a sort of primal urge to either run from whatever was hunting or to submit and die quickly.

Specs of blood, made blue by its spectral hue, flew from the spook's broken maw as it yelled.

It flew at me like a torpedo.

I tried to spin and swing Baby upwards in a vertical slice, but the spook got to me first while my sword's point was still facing the floor. It hit me in a tackle, still howling like a wild boar. My legs buckled and I fell with the spook. It dug its gnarled fingers into my hair — some digits missing, some just nubs, others with nails like daggers. Tears welled as it scratched my scalp, nearly drawing blood. I swung Baby in a tiny, horizontal slash using just my wrists, nicking the spook's thigh. It shrieked then threw me into the wall.

Most of my air left me as I hit. I slid to the ground, gasping but reaching back and grabbing my shotgun. The spook flew at me before I could fully draw it, but I was ready this time; I stuck Baby out, point first, just like I had when he'd been inside of Beefman — though this time a stab through its ghostly gut would undoubtedly Sever it. The spook showed a surprising amount of cognizance and stopped midway through its flight, staring at my sword. It looked entranced by the Blade, and was clearly confident that I wouldn't be able to reach and harm it from this distance.

Ah, am I ever underestimated.

Shells zipped into the shotty, the same ones I'd used against Charlie, and fired out just as quickly. I hardly needed to aim. It was all instinctual at this point.

Glowing blue bullets slammed into the spook, throwing it backwards like a sack of flour. Its howls of rage turned into those of pain, then into sad whimpers as it slammed onto the kitchen counter. Even still, it reached towards me wildly as I neared its resting form. I popped another shot into its head. The spook recoiled, head flying backwards so fiercely that I expected its neck to snap from the momentum alone, but it somehow remained in our realm. *That's some impressive resilience.* I stood above the monster, Baby's radiant tip pointing at his pig snout. The spook's pebble-sized black eyes stared at the Blade... almost longingly. Desperate, pained whimpers rattled his throat.

Its eyes rolled and locked with mine; they looked sad, a glint of humanity tucked away deep inside them. It let out a sigh, like a tired dog's.

Then it actually spoke.

"Please..." it gurgled, barely audible. It was almost entirely dependent on the shape of its mouth and the rasping breath to enunciate its words — like its vocal cords were shot or otherwise removed. It took a deep, struggling breath. "Please... kill... kill me."

I flinched, shocked. It wasn't often that I found a spook who *wanted* to pass on; I mean, if they really wanted to leave, they just *could.* What was so different with this guy?

When it comes to spooks, things should be easy. Hunting should be no more than finding ravenous, murderous beasts and taking them down. I liked that way: simple. Keeps my head clear, lets my arms do the work.

Since entering that mansion — from the strangely cognizant and reasonable Charlie to this weirdly suicidal monstrosity — things had moved *away* from simple. And I wasn't a fan.

Either way, who was I to ignore a man-monster-pig-thing's dying-but-not-dying request? I reeled back, and cleanly took the spook's head from his shoulders, Severing it. The head rolled realistically onto the ground. A single lonely tear rolled down its lumpy cheek. It let out a surprisingly human sigh of relief, then both head and body faded away.

"Um..." Gus said. "That was kinda weird... right?"

"Yeah. I'd say it was."

We stared at where the strange spook had died, silent for a moment.

Silent except for the ever-present hum, raucous and looming and... disappointing.

"You hear that," Gus said. It wasn't a question.

I sighed. "I fucking hear it. But it's no longer my problem."

Gus looked at me. "But what about Jennifer? If she comes back here, she could be in serious danger! Whatever's haunting this place could come out and kill her easily."

"Yup. And it wouldn't be my responsibility."

Gus scowled silently.

"Don't give me that," I snarled back. "I've already saved her once. I'm here to kill shit and get paid, not save every damsel that falls in my lap. Oh, and what's next on the agenda? Two more chicks in desperate need of Graves' help. Well, I've helped too many chicks and gotten too little ass, if you ask me." Gus didn't reply. "You're lucky they're paying," I continued. "Now hike up your panties and grab your little box. Time's-a-wastin'."

The Garcias' place was downtown, in a decrepit apartment complex surrounded by decrepit apartment complexes. Homeless and drug-full folks decorated the chipped sidewalk sandwiching the street. We parked the van in the sizeable lot attached to the building, right next to Jessie's blue Sedan.

Gus and I frowned in silence as we entered and traversed the complex, observing the denizens of downtown Hartsville as they went about their daily lives. One lady sat in a ratty chair in the lobby, her head bobbing listlessly, her eyes staring into nothing. Another dude crossed his flabby arms and glared us down. A noticeable bulge in his pocket told me he was armed. A guy nearby the Garcias' apartment was so still he looked dead; foam bubbled and rolled down his chin.

Dreary voices filtered through the apartment's door. Gus knocked politely and we waited until a few dozen locks along the door's seam were clicked open methodically. It was pulled open by a lean Mexican kid wearing a wife-beater and loose jeans. A thin dark mustache painted his upper lip, prepubescent and desperate to prove itself. The kid stared at me with dark-brown eyes.

"You're back," he said. "Both of you."

"We are," Gus said. "And I promise we'll do the job right this time. May we come in, Tony?"

He kept staring at me, arm and thin body blocking the open doorway. "I don't trust him," Tony said simply.

"It's just a shotgun, kid," I said, crossing my arms and shrugging. "I was doing my job, nothing more or less."

"You were going to kill my abuelita."

"I was going to *save* your abuelita. I was gonna kill the *ghost*."

He scoffed, then finally broke his glare and switched to Gus. "You can vouch for this guy?"

Gus didn't reply at first, which surprised me and pissed me off at once, but eventually, he said, "I do. Even if I didn't, I'm not sure we can help your grandma without him."

Tony nodded and — after a short silence — beckoned us inside.

The apartment was nice and homey, small yet comfy, stuffed yet well-kept. The couches and chairs were old and dusty and pillowy as clouds, covered with patches and one with plastic. Catholic iconography hung symmetrically and neatly along the chipped sheetrock. The floor was carpet, kept stunningly clean and brilliantly white. In the living room was a blocky CRT, playing an old soap opera in which a very handsome couple yelled at each other in Spanish, the noise clipped and muffled by the TV's ancient speakers. In front of that sat an old woman with leathery brown skin, bleach-white hair, and loose-hanging flesh. She stared unendingly at the soap opera, her entire body as still as a statue.

To the left was a small kitchenette, pots and pans hanging throughout its entire circumference. A pair of young women stood behind the counter, looking at us with vastly different expressions.

Jessie had her bushy brown hair tied behind her head in a shrub-like sphere of fuzz, unmasking her charmingly plump face. She wore loose-fitting clothing — though still not loose enough to disguise her delightfully rounded chest and hips. Her glasses masked her eyes, but her frown was more concerned than it was angry or judging.

The other woman's hair fell in silken strings to her shoulders, dyed so silver it was nearly white. Her skin was pale as moonlight, and her lips were painted a matching shade of metallic silver. A leather jacket draped around her shoulders and fell to her waist, unzipped and surrounding her small and perky breasts – both cupped behind her pink shirt. She wore leather pants that hugged her hips, her pale white midriff exposed between her shirt and pants. From one hip hung a sharp saber, fed through a loop attached to her belt.

In her crystal-blue eyes was only malice.

"*You*," the young woman said. I couldn't tell who she was staring at, me or the nervously stammering Gus.

I spread my hands and grinned jovially. "Me."

Her gaze dripped icy mist as she met mine. "Didn't you already screw this up enough?"

"Nah," I said. "I think it could use a little more screwing, if you get me."

She grimaced. "You're not welcome here. Take your sword and get out." A hand draped calmly over her saber's hilt. "I'll make this ugly if I have to."

Jessie squeezed the other woman's thin arm. "Emily—"

"What?" I chuckled. "You gonna fend me off with that meat thermometer?"

Emily's lip curled in a defensive snarl.

"H-hey," Gus said, raising his arms. "Let's j-just cool it, okay?"

Emily's frozen glare shifted. "I thought I told you to stand down, Gus. You're not needed. You'll only get in the way."

Gus wilted. His clammy, full-moon face fell as he stared at his shoes. Ridiculously, ludicrously, I felt defensive for the sad dweeb.

"Oh, and you guys are making such astounding fucking progress," I snapped, gesturing back towards the granny. The old woman had registered none of the conversation; she sat like a gargoyle, a quilt draped over her tiny lap. Tony sat next to her and looked with worried eyes.

"More than you did," Emily said.

This little dog sure has a lot of bite, don't she? "Oh yeah? And what progress is that?"

"We, um... she groaned..." Jessie said with little confidence.

"She groaned," I repeated. "Cool. Is that all? If you got her to fucking *groan* then I guess we can just wrap this shit up and call it day, huh?" The girls glared at me.

"What happens when you try to exorcise her, Jessie?" Gus asked, voice silent, as if he were trying to avoid Emily's wrath.

"That's when she groaned. Mrs. Garcia is completely unresponsive otherwise."

"I remember." Gus's tone held a tiny cube of freezing ice.

He looked at Emily with mild disdain, a beta-male, scornful of his alpha, and Jessie with open longing, yet hurt and hostility and jealousy and...

Teenagers.

"What was your plan from here?" Gus asked.

"*Was?*" Emily leaned off the counter. "You act like we're off the case — which we're not. Go take your tools somewhere else, Gus. And you," she pointed a shining silver nail at me, "leave. Before I make you."

Strike two, I thought.

"Em, I think we *do* need their help. Gus has always had a... a way with the ghosts. I think, I don't know, maybe he could get through to Mrs. Garcia." Jessie looked at her partner desperately.

Emily sniffed. "What does he have that we don't?"

Frowning, Gus dug into his backpack and pulled out the Spetrenchancing Squaredroid — or whatever the fuck it was called. "This will capture the ghost the moment it leaves Mrs. Garcia's body. It won't be able to escape. Trust me."

"Bull," Emily said.

"That's right, girlfriend," I laughed. "Gus just made you *obsolete!*"

Gus, in all chubby, clammy, sweater-vested glory, cracked a small grin, aimed directly at Emily. "I think we've got it from here."

"Ha! How are you going to get the ghost *out* of Mrs. Garcia, stupid?" Emily countered eloquently. "You need an exorcist for that. And Jessie leaves when *I* leave."

"I'll figure that out," Gus said. "We don't need *you two,* that's for sure." He said it with more venom than he meant to, flinching right after the words left his mouth. Jessie frowned down at him, brows pinched.

"Whatever," Emily spat. "I'm not leaving. You and your

boyfriend can sit back and watch us if you really want to, but you won't touch Mrs. Garcia."

I took a lunging step towards Emily, puffing my chest out and staring down at her blue eyes. "And just what the fuck are going to do to stop me, hot stuff?"

Her teeth flashed between thin, blue-painted lips. "I'll stab this *thermometer* right through your heart, asshole."

And strike three.

Taking a small step back, I reached and cleanly pulled Baby from her sheath. The angels sang, her radiance caressed the room, and her steel hummed in my ear like a sweet lullaby. Sneering, Emily whipped out her own weapon with a swirl of flashy metal. The blade was so thin and sharp I thought it could floss through one of my pores. The hilt was brown leather, the handguard a gilded gold. Small metal lightning bolts etched along the sides of the curving metal. A blue glow — dulled compared to Baby's holy light — coated the entire saber.

"*Emily, no!*" Jessie said.

"*Graves, stop!*" Gus yelled.

"Stay out of it," me and Emily growled in unison.

"*EEEAAAIIIIICCCHHH,*" something screeched.

Blotting Emily out of my thoughts, I turned on my heel and faced the sudden sound. Abuelita Garcia had stood out from her chair, no longer concerned with her show. Her white hair was in disarray, strands coming undone and falling this way and that. The old woman's tight mouth twitched into a sneer. Drool leaked from her maw, dribbling and dropping onto the carpet. Mrs. Garcia's eyes glowed a blinding blue.

"She's *up*?" Jessie cried.

"Fuck yeah, she's up," I replied, pointing Baby's tip at the old woman. Mrs. Garcia's humongous eyes were glued to the Blade's sheening surface; I waggled her around, and the old woman's sight followed like a cat's on a string. She clacked her yellow teeth hungrily.

"A-Abuelita?" Tony said, moving beside Mrs. Garcia and placing a hand on her bony shoulder. "What's going on? Are you okay—" The old woman swung her arm back without looking, hitting her grandson's chest. She swatted Tony like you would a mote of dust. He flew backwards and hit the wall, *hard*. The plaster cracked like a sheet of frost.

"*ShhhhRRREEEAAHHH,*" she screamed again, hands gripping and clenching repeatedly.

"Still think you don't need my sword?" I shouted.

Then I flew to take the old woman's head off.

Chapter 14

Professionals

I can be a delicate kind of man. In the bedroom, I've been called a *generous lover*; I make sure that the woman has had her fill of pleasantries well before I've had mine, touching and probing for her weak spots until I've earned her fiercest reactions — then I go in for the climax. I went about fighting Abuelita Garcia in a similar sort of way.

Minus the cunnalingus, obviously.

She aimed a bony-knuckled punch at my face, but I deftly leaned to the side. The fist *wooshed* on by, whistling as if shot from a cannon. I gave her a punch of my own, right in the ribs — a test of her resilience — to absolutely no reaction; Abuelita Garcia's stance hardly even shifted. The old woman threw a sledgehammering fist at the back of my head. I juked just in time, then snarled and returned the favor; my hand *cracked* as it crashed into her wrinkly, angled face. A wave of searing pain shot through my hand and arm... but Abuelita Garcia reacted only with a glare of wild malice.

Her rock-hard forehead *rushed* forward, and in my pained distraction I hadn't prepared a dodge. Stars exploded in my sight as our skulls met. My knees buckled under me. I fell on my ass, disoriented and vulnerable. The old lady, shrieking like a deranged banshee, leapt on top of me and punched my chest with gorilla-like slams.

Air left me with each blow. "*Jesus. CHRIST! What. THE*

FUCK!"

In a blur of silver, something nicked Abuelita Garcia on the arm. A spurt of blood rocketed out, painting her pink sleeve and the bleach-white carpet with red. She recoiled and jumped away from me, far more deftly than any old woman should've been able. Emily whipped her tiny blade around, cleaning the blood from it in thin splashes.

Blue mist crawled from Abuelita Garcia's pores and caressed her fresh wound, drying blood and closing flesh instantaneously.

Now that *looks familiar, don't it...*

"Graves!" Gus yelled. He and Jessie were in the kitchenette, staring at the old woman with open horror. "Is that what I think it is?"

"If you're thinking 'we're fucking fucked,' you might just be right."

"If this is the same specter as earlier... do you know what that means?"

"Yeah, I'm aware."

"What are you two—" Emily didn't get to finish that thought, as Mrs. Garcia suddenly registered her as an actual threat. The old woman leapt at the younger with a disproportionate grace, easily ducking under the saber's quick jab and wrapping her bone-thin arms around Emily's waist. "Jessie!" she yelled. "Exorcise her! *Now!"* Abuelita Garcia was attached to the hunter like an opossum to its mother.

Jessie looked terrified, but she shakily stood and shuffled next to the scrambling pair all the same. Hands trembling, she dug in her pocket and pulled out a thick glove, padding bulging from the palm. She slipped it on, swallowing, and brought her gloved hand up, facing the ravenous old woman. Jessie's palm turned a dull blue, visible even through the dense black glove.

"*Don't!*" Gus yelled. But the girls ignored him, focused on their task. "If you let the ghost out, it'll—"

A wind whipped through the small apartment, like our own miniature hurricane, cutting off Gus' words with a sharp knife of air. Paintings banged against the walls, papers went flying like fluttering birds, dust and dirt were pulled from each crevice and sent spiraling out into the open. Jessie was the eye of this storm, debris and filth swirling around her in a wide tornado as she exorcised the old woman.

"Fucking *no!*" I yelled, but the shout was pulled from my lips and added to the winds.

Blue light leaked from Abueltia Garcia, who was still clinging to Emily's waist as the young hunter swiveled and thrashed. She seemed hesitant to stab the old woman with her weapon — she would've known better if I could've spoken to her. Beams of light exploded out of the old woman's eyes and mouth as if she were a jack-o-lantern. Her bestial shrieks melted into guttural shouts, like a lion's roar mixed with a dying man's. The trio of lights brightened and brightened, until they *popped* and condensed into a roiling blue fog. The dense mist rolled down the old woman's face, pooling on the floor and spreading in clouds. Finally, Mrs. Garcia's limbs and head went limp, and her grip around Emily's hips slackened. The hunter lowered her to the ground gently, both of them encased in the blue fog. The glow on Jessie's glove dimmed. She put her hands on her knees and panted, exhausted.

The hum roared, stemming from where Mrs. Garcia lay. Emily, silent and alert, backed away from the blue clouds and back towards Jessie. The exorcist touched the scythe's shoulder worriedly. Emily brought her hand up and patted Jessie's.

That's when the fog coagulated.

At first, it formed into the vague shape of the ghostly grotesque we'd fought earlier... but then it changed. Rather than a mismatched maw stuffed with jagged, broken teeth, the thing's jaws extended three times and sprouted fangs the size of daggers, and just as sharp. Its arms went from simply meaty to disproportionately wide and lumped with tough muscle. Glowing organs burst from the thing's chest and stomach; slimy intestines and lungs and a heart leaked from it like jelly, until the viscera hardened and formed a red plate of blood-pumping armor. Its legs shrunk and emptied into its body, eventually becoming only sagging bags of hollow flesh. It towered over us now, its torso growing and elongating. Two bulging eyes rolled across its tight flesh. They reached the sides of its head and stopped, staring emotionlessly all around the small apartment.

"Oh, you fucking morons," I growled.

"The hell!?" Emily yelled, reaching back and hugging Jessie with one arm.

"You seem confused. Let me explain: You two just fucked us, and probably everyone else in this town." A sharp pink tongue lolled out of the thing's mouth. Its bugging eyes flicked between each of us.

Then its eyes fell on me, and the Blade in my hand.

The beast's fist thumped on the carpet as he moved towards me, otherwise silent as a stalking lion. Its legs dangled sickeningly behind it; it was walking just using its meaty arms. Teeth flashed when it opened its gator-like maw, letting loose a whispering scream.

I met the monster halfway. Shadows danced as Baby twirled. Grunting, I went to slice at the corrupted spook's wide chest — just a testing cut, that's all I wanted. Instead, Baby bounced off the monster's savage parry, swatted away with the back of its hand like a fly. This fly branded a savage burn into the spook's limb in just that short time, but that only pissed it off. The beast shrieked again. Wildly, imprecisely, a fist the size of my entire torso came to meet me. Panicked, I brought Baby up to block.

Block she did, but physics are physics and I was knocked right off my feet. I blasted through the kitchen counter — right between the ladies — then *crashed* into the plaster wall. The spook wasn't done yet; before I could get the breath back in my lungs and the spinning stars back into space, another set of knuckles met Baby's steel. Her metal rang like a gong, and I was pushed one foot deeper into the dusty plaster. In came another punch, then another, then another, each like its own chugging train.

Finally, after shards of plaster and torn metal framing had scraped dozens of slits into my jumpsuit and skin, I *exploded* out of the wall, dust spilling around me as if I were covered in chalk.

Inside this new apartment was a pot-bellied white dude with crooked yellow teeth, and a woman breastfeeding her now squalling baby. Both leapt up and shrieked as I entered their apartment. Giant fists still met Baby's steel, threatening to push me through the carpeted floor as if it were made from glass.

Time to try something stupid; growling and grunting, I used my right arm to hold Baby and shield myself from the repeated punches — which were getting no weaker — and used my left to pull out the shotty. My ribs cracked — again — and a terrible pain rocketed up my leg in a stream of liquid fire as the hardly perturbed assault continued. All air left me. I banged the gun on the corrupted spook's snout, popping open the chamber and loading it instantly. The shells were pure, blinding white, buzzing and humming as they entered the sawed-off. I reached back to put some distance from the spook's face, then fired. Light *erupted* from the shotgun's barrel. The monster's tiny pupils shrank further with the flash. It clawed at its eyes, stumbling backwards and back into the Garcias' abode.

I pointed at my new roommates. "You two," I groaned, gripping my chest — and my *leg*, *my leg*. "Get the fuck outta here. Go tell everyone on this floor to do the same — everyone in the whole *complex*." Terrified, they ran out of the apartment, hopefully to do what I'd instructed.

I expected to find the Specter Detectors either dead or locked in combat with the corrupted spook, but the fucking thing was still focused on *me*, even through its blind confusion.

"The fuck did *I* do?" I asked no one.

Slowly but surely, the spook was regaining its sight. Its pathetic whimpers were becoming enraged growls.

"Emily — Em — whatever the fuck your name is, distract it while I fight."

"M-me?" The silver-haired girl looked more a child than a 19-year-old, stumbling over her words as she stared at the looming beast. "I just... I don't—"

"Oh, what? Not so confident anymore?" I said. "Relax. The thing has a raging hard-on for me, for some fucking reason, so it'll only cave your head in if *after* I die. Probably."

The girl swallowed. "O... Okay. Just tell me what to do."

I did not sign up to be a fucking babysitter. But I said, "Just slice the thing in a million different places. I'll deal the major blows, but I can't while he's trying to squish me." The scythe nodded, pale hand clenching her saber's hilt desperately.

In my lifetime — both before and after I became a hunter — I've fought a lot of big things. Ghosts, demons, monsters, a lot of them choose brawn over brains. That has its merits, definitely, but the bigger they are, the bigger they fall — or whatever. And that fall will be all the easier if they're attacking without a thought; they're predictable, open, vulnerable despite the bulging muscle and enormous strength. This guy wasn't any different.

Except I had a set of broken ribs and a leg barely functioning. Every movement was filled with a sharp agony, a hundred little daggers tearing apart my insides.

Gasping, I jumped out of the way of one of the spook's downward punches. The wood underneath the carpet *cracked*, the cloth above it now hanging as limply as flesh over a mushed skull. Emily, shaky and unpracticed in brawling with this kind of thing, sliced the monster clean across the elbow — a bug bite. It hardly seemed to register a thing; another boulder-sized fist flew at me. Screaming in pain, I parried the fist, Baby's steel singing.

"Stop pussyfooting!" I shouted. *Fuck my leg, my LEG.* "Stab, slice, cut — I don't give a fuck, just make it notice you."

Shaking like a leaf, Emily twirled on her heeled boots and sent a shining slash at the thing's back. Sure enough, the strike was true; the corrupted spook *howled*, mist rising over its massive shoulders, then turned towards the girl.

Grinning despite my throbbing leg, I held my Blade next to my head and ran at the thing's back. Baby stabbed through its flesh like a fork through meat. Radiant steam *exploded* out of the spook's shoulders, a fountain of glowing blue blood. Just in time; the spook had had its fist ready to pulverize Emily like a walnut, and she was frozen still in her terror.

Even more mist burst forth after I pulled Baby from the spook's ghostly flesh. "Gus!" I shouted. "You know what to do. Get on with it!"

"Oh!" was all he said. He was standing in front of Jessie

with his arms trembling yet outstretched, protecting the exorcist in Emily's place. *How fucking sweet.*

"You," I pointed at the scythe, who was stone-still and staring wide-eyed at the slavering monster, "keep nicking. The more injuries we can make, the easier this'll be for Gus." She said nothing, did nothing, looked nowhere but at the corrupted spook. I grabbed a pillow off the couch and chucked it at her. "*Now!*" I yelled as the cushion bashed Emily in the head. She snapped out of her shock, shook her silver hair, then went to work.

I'll admit, it was impressive stuff. Emily was not a novice — far from it. She darted in and out of the monster's reach, slicing when she could and dodging when she couldn't, each move precise and elegant despite her skin-tight pants. Her saber flashed out like a frog's tongue, cutting and dicing just as fast. Sometimes Emily would have to pause and catch her breath, or she would come close to stumbling in her retreats, but those were failings tempered out of any swordsman as they trained. Maybe I was ten times the fighter at her age, but I had some advantages.

Still, I wouldn't let her have all the fun.

Emily's saber may have been good for making infinite papercuts, but Baby was good for *chopping* — maiming, goring, delimbing — and that's just what this big boy needed. She bit into the corrupted spook's elbow, slicing through dead flesh and *crunching* into bone like an axe into wood. The spook toppled, but not before I finished the cut; his giant, swollen arm fell to the side, spurting translucent blood. Dozens of straight yet true, short yet deep slices were taken from every inch of its body. Mist surrounded it like a ship at night. With a savage grunt, I brought Baby down on the thing's monstrously thick neck. Blood *exploded* outwards with unnatural pressure, strong enough to peel paint from the walls.

And the thing was far from dead.

"Alright, Gus. Get to it," I said, wrenching Baby out of the spurting wound.

Gus' little box had whirred to life minutes ago, so he was ready for my command; the thick mist spun in a cyclone of radiant blue, rushing towards the shaking medium. The corrupted spook flopped onto his back and screeched towards the ceiling as it was dragged. A meaty paw made to grab me, but I plunged Baby through the back of its hand and pinned it there. The hand was ripped from its wrist as the beast was sucked away. Emily, cold and silent, thrust her saber through the monster's eye, earning further howls.

Eventually, finally, the corrupted spook vanished within the Cuboid. The sudden silence was filled with our ragged breaths and the notable absence of the hum.

"Gus, *that's* what you've been working on?" Jessie said, crawling out from behind the counter. "It's... the ghost, it's in there?"

"Yes," was all he could manage. The bulb was filled and glowing, just as it had been earlier.

"Oh... oh my God. M-Mr. Graves!" Jessie suddenly squeaked, pointing at my leg.

Something white and rock hard protruded from my jumpsuit, trails of red droplets running along its length and dribbling onto the carpet, which soaked up the blood like a tampon. Through my hazy pain, it took me minutes to realize what I was looking at.

"Okay," I said. "What kinda food do they have in that kitchen."

Some time passed — seconds, I think — all in a whir of senseless agony. The next time my brain took over, I was feasting on uncooked dough and crunchy beans, shoveling the raw food in my mouth by the handful. Jessie looked worriedly at my leg while Gus and Emily argued by the counter. Someone had propped Mrs. Garcia back on the couch, and Tony was cradling her in his scrawny arms.

There was a sudden and sharp pain in my leg, where Jessie had poked, testing. "Buzz off," I growled. Then, as the young exorcist straightened, I *banged* my leg against the counter, resetting the bone with a *crack*. I gritted my teeth nearly to dust to keep myself from screaming, a tingling, pinching pain squirming up my body.

Sputtering, Jessie went to join in conversation with the other Specter Detectors. I waddled over and searched the fridge for more food, having exhausted the sack of raw beans. To my absolute delight, I found a pair of T-bone steaks. The meat was tender and juicy when my teeth gnawed through it. The steer's raw, dead flesh squirted cooled blood down my throat. I shivered in ecstasy as my leg was dutifully healed.

The three hunters were staring at me — Gus' eyes wide, Jessie's fearful, and Emily's disgusted. I pictured myself: Thin blood leaking from my maw and down my pale skin, the slurping and crunching noises as I tore apart the remaining bone.

"What?" I said, swallowing the red meat. "Gotta make do with what you've got." The second steak was just as juicy.

My leg half-healed and supporting a bit of my weight, I hobbled over to say my farewells. "You two certainly bungled that shit up, didn't you."

"*Us*?" Emily cried. "Without Jessie the ghost would still be inside Mrs. Garcia! The hell would *you* have done differently?"

"Didn't you see what Gus' device did? That coulda happened with a *tenth* as much trouble if you kids hadn't gotten ahead of yourselves."

"But you might have *killed* Mrs. Garcia!"

"I can be precise if I need to — unlike you, *Em*. You talk a big fucking talk, but the second shit got real you were shaking like Parker McParkensons in the Arctic fucking Sea."

"Th-that's—"

"That's exactly right, and you fucking know it. You two are *lucky* I showed up."

"*Lucky!?*" Jessie's head swung up. "Look at the damage you've caused!" She pointed towards the gaping hole in the plaster, then the sobbing Tony and his unconscious abuelita. "This never would've happened if you hadn't shown up."

"And the old woman woulda been better off as a host for that fuckin' monster?" I shouted. "Get real. And after you do that, clean this shit up and send me my goddamn money."

"Money? The hell are you talking about?" Emily asked.

"Oh, you'd best not try to skimp out on me, ladies. I'll get that money, no matter what—"

"We're not being paid for this job," Jessie said, brows raised with incredulity. "This was to pay off a debt."

"Yeah, we... screwed up a case a few months back," Emily explained. "Mr. Hostephony was kind enough to—"

"*Fuck!*" I yelled. "That slimy little shit has his toes dipped in every pot, don't he? *Goddamn fuck!*" Snarling, I spun and faced Gus. "If you knew about this, Gus, I swear to baby Christ I'll—"

"I didn't! I swear!" He put his hands up defensively. Then he turned towards the girls. "You two took *another* case without me? And you didn't even tell me...?"

Jessie looked at her shoes, abashed. Emily stared flatly at the medium, but the curling of her thin mouth gave away her guilt.

Gus scoffed in disbelief. "S-some group we are." His voice cracked as he held back tears. "No w-wonder you two messed up your last case." Gus' brow suddenly furrowed, his fists clenched. "You *need* me. And you know what? You're gonna have to survive without me."

Emily flinched. "What do you mean?"

"I mean Graves and I have a case to finish — one that we *haven't* ruined. You two *have fun*," he choked out. "While we'll go be professionals."

The medium turned to leave, glowing Cuboid in hand. A round droplet fell from his eye as he blinked profusely. Jessie looked on the verge of tears herself, while Emily just seemed confused and angry at once.

Fucking teenagers.

"What was the deal with that ghost?" the scythe asked suddenly. "Why was it so, I don't know, mutated?"

"Its haunt is Jennifer's mansion. I'm not sure why or how the fuck it got so far away, nor am I sure that I want to find out."

"So it was corrupted?" Jessie asked.

I nodded. "Do you understand how fucked you two were now?" They didn't reply. My mouth twisted. "Gus saved both your asses," I growled. "You owe him. And, more importantly, you owe *me*. I won't forget this. If you know what's good for you, you won't either." I turned to leave.

"Wait! Let... let us help!" Emily yelled after me.

"Ha! Not in a million fuckin' years." Looking over my shoulder, I said, "Go back to your little headquarters and think about what you've done." That seemed to set Emily on fire; she visibly grinded her teeth, and her hands clenched so hard her skin squeaked.

Smiling, I left them to clean up the mess.

Chapter 15

Haggard

The spook hardly fought as Baby entered and exited its bulbous neck. It looked nearly identical to its brother — we were back at the mansion, so the corruption had melted away — but the lumps were in different places and it'd retained most of its teeth. The light sheened off the metal plate drilled into its skull.

The spook sighed in relief, then faded away, head severed and rolling.

And the hum was loud as ever.

Gus frowned. "Graves, there has to be something you're not telling me."

I shrugged nonchalantly. "Whatever do you mean?"

"Those ghosts were far from normal; they were all mutated and disfigured, and that was *without* being corrupted." He rubbed his chins, thinking. "And on that subject, why did this guy fly so far from his haunt? That's rare, Graves. You know it is."

"What's it matter now? The case is through. Time to pack it in and wait for Jenny to wake up and pay me."

"But, the hum..."

"I repeat: Not my fuckin' problem," I said.

"It could be." Gus seemed more ponderous than argumentative. "If there are more of those things haunting this place, then more of them could flee and become corrupted. That would be catastrophic, even for you. In fact... we may want to bring the rest of the Union in on this—"

"And split the pay? Ha!"

"Is it really all about the money for you?"

"Yes," I replied instantly. "I've already sliced my pay in half with Josephi, not to mention the money and time I just lost helping your girlfriends. I'd rather let this whole town burn to cinders than sacrifice another goddamn *cent.*"

Gus grimaced at me. "If that's the case, then consider this: If you abandon this case, the Union will show up regardless. You can only hide it for so long, even shorter if each ghost here is corrupted. It would mean chaos and blood; that's something the Union can't ignore."

Fuck... the medium was right. Wrapping up at that point would mean a possible *army* of beefed-up spooks thrashing through Hartsville, killing and destroying and burning. The Union would show up, realize that I'd knowingly allowed it to happen, then rip every coin from my horde anyway. *I have to see this bullshit to the end*, I thought, sighing.

Gus was still waiting for an explanation; he knew he had me, the bloody fucker.

I told him about everything: The underground cells, my battle with Charlie, the secret laboratory, the malformed remains and Charlie's reaction to finding them. Gus listened attentively, nodding once or twice.

"And then that guy chucked me out the fuckin' window," I said. "I woke up and decided that I needed a medium to help me track the spook down, so I went and grabbed you." I spread my hands, gesturing around the destroyed kitchen. "Hilarity ensued."

Gus made a noncommittal noise. "Is that it?"

"Oh, and I went and *talked* with Josephi this morning. He gave me this address and said it had something to do with the case." I pulled the paper from a pocket and handed it to him. "Though he couldn't say why or how."

Gus scanned the paper, then his eyebrows shot up.

"What is it?" I asked.

He fished in his pocket and pulled out a smartphone, rapidly typing on its keyboard. "That's what I thought. This is the address of a maximum-security prison just out of state."

"What the hell does that have to do with this haunt? I swear to God if Josephi tried to send me on a goose chase..."

Gus squinted at the paper, contemplative. "Unless..."

"Unless what?"

"Unless the previous owner of this mansion is being held there."

I frowned at him. "Erick Horst," I said. He nodded. "The guy'd have to be well over a fuckin' hundred."

Gus shrugged. "People have been alive longer."

As much as I wanted to doubt it, an online search told us that Erick was alive and well, and had been imprisoned for nearly eighty years. Josephi had given us an absolute *well* of knowledge in the form of an ancient inmate — how kind of him.

Not only that, but he'd presented me a straight-up fucking Nazi on a silver platter. I've done my fair share of fucked up shit, but — dare I say — I would *never* be able catch up with someone who'd willingly participated in the genocide of millions of innocents.

I now had the best host your average degenerate could ask for!

"Now continue straight for three-quarters of a mile," I said.

"You're sure?" Gus tried to lean over and double-check, but his wheels rumbled on the gravel, over the side of the asphalt road, and he quickly corrected his steering.

"Uh." I squinted at Gus' smartphone, trying to make sense of all the colored lines and tiny icons used in its GPS app. "Pretty sure, yeah."

"Because you've taken us down seven wildly incorrect roads now."

"*Keep straight*," said the phone's feminine, sensual yet playful voice.

Jesus, I thought, *I'm horny for fucking A.I. now.*

We were driving through a forest comprised of narrow, vein-like roads worming every which way. Rain sprinkled around; Gus' wipers arched across the windshield every so often. The sun — filtered through roiling clouds — was well past its crest, its light streaming through treetops as if they were blinded windows.

Tik-tok, tik-tok.

I frowned at the otherworldly phone. "Hey, I'm not great with this shit. I— oh, there it is."

"Where?" Gus said, already panicked. "Which road?"

"It's... uh..."

"*Turn left now*," the phone screamed.

Gus turned. *Hard.* Tires skidded along the road as the van's rear veered, falling behind its front wheels. Rainwater fountained from his wheels. He got us going straight again — after some screams of panic. He looked nervously and accusingly at me, but I was too focused on the building in front of us, rising out of the foliage, to notice.

Haggard Prison was more a castle than a supermax facility; it towered higher than most buildings I'd seen in person, including Jennifer's mansion. It was mostly made with old, moss-riddled brick — some had chipped, broken, or fallen off. The only things that told me it was a prison were the barbed wire fence surrounding it and the bars driven through the windows that randomly decorated its walls. There was one of those toll-booth kinda things by the only opening in the fence, a large striped bar falling in front of it and blocking our entrance. A short, dark-skinned lady was running it, dressed in an outfit denoting a security officer. Through the window, I saw her take her feet down and mark the book she was reading as we drove up.

"Hello," Gus said, after rolling his window down, "we were hoping to meet with someone today — Erick Horst. Is he, uh, still around?"

The security lady raised her eyebrows and looked him up and down. "You ain't one of those Neo-Nazi types, are you?" she asked, accent southern and tone unamused.

"Uh, we're not, no. Just wanted to ask him some questions for a... project."

The security guard studied him some more — Gus gave her what I assumed was his most charming smile — then she pressed a little button attached to a speaker on her desk. "We got a pair of boys who want to meet the Nazi," she said into the mic.

"Really?" a male voice whined through the speaker. "Alright, I guess. Send 'em through."

She pressed a different button and the bar swung upwards. Gus nodded his thanks, then we drove forward and parked in the impressively empty lot. A guy with a pump-action shotgun stood next to the front entrance, staring at us with bored indifference.

Haggard's insides were still brick-lined and in a losing battle with the forest around them; moss and dirt littered its brick floor, various kinds of little bugs crawled around, hiding between bricks and in the wall. A few more guards were posted in this meeting area, guarding only empty cells and randomly placed tables. One guard, a burly guy with a handlebar mustache, opened a rusty metal door next to him and said, "Go ahead and wait in here." I recognized his voice from the tollbooth's speaker.

It was a small room — brick-encased like the rest of the prison — almost devoid of decoration, other than a rectangular table in its center, another metal door on the far wall, and a barred window to our left. The guard stood in the doorway and quickly mumbled into a walkie-talkie Velcroed to a strap on his shoulder. A loud buzz blasted from the door across from us, then it swung open slowly, screaming on its hinges.

An extremely old man shuffled through the doorway. Horst's wrists and ankles were chained together, chain pulled taut with each trembling step, his breath coming ragged from moving that short distance. His nose was bulbous and red, his ears droopy, head bald and covered with liver spots. Horst shook as he sat across from us, sighing a relieved and tired breath.

"30 minutes." The guard slammed the door and left us alone with the ancient Nazi.

Horst looked up at us through a shelf-like brow thickened with age. Sad wheezes sucked through his wrinkled mouth, each breath laborious and painful, as if they were being filtered through fiberglass. His eyes said that he'd lived longer than even *he* had hoped. The poor, miserable, pathetic old man.

Gus decided to break the silence. "Um, good afternoon, Mr. Horst. How are you doing?"

He wheezed and struck Gus with a tired glare.

"Not so great, I take it?" I asked pleasantly.

Another wheeze.

"D'awww. That's too bad, baby boy. Wanna sit on Daddy's lap? Maybe get a good burping?"

"Graves... what are you doing?" Gus asked.

"Nazi, remember? We got pretty much free reign to bully this dude."

Erick huffed out a scornful laugh. "What is it you want from me." His accent was perfectly American, though I assumed he could switch it back to German as easily as pulling a trigger.

"We're wondering what you'd been doing at your mansion over in Hartsville when our side caught you," Gus said. "Other than trading our secrets, I mean."

Horst squinted at us, then rolled his head back and let out a throaty, rich laugh, filled with decades of hateful placidity — of a bitter lifetime rotting in jail, anger his only company, forced to put on a calm face to preserve the dignity of his Reich.

The laugh died down, then his eyes turned teary and wistful. "Something terrible," he croaked. "Something ingenious. Wicked. Horrifying..." He swallowed, looking past us in remembrance. "*Beautiful.*"

"Alright," I said after a silence. "But what the hell *was* it? And before you try and keep it from us—"

"Soldiers." Horst's beady eyes finally met mine. "Soldiers more *powerful* than any our nations had ever seen — more than any soldier found on this Earth. Even the Führer was impressed." His accent tilted more towards German as he wound down, a twinkle of pride in his eye.

"Like, *super-soldiers*?" Gus asked.

"More than that, I'd hope." His loose jowls spread around a surprisingly wide, toothless smile. "*Gods*," he whispered.

"And how were you crafting up these 'gods.' I assume it's got something to do with the labs hidden around your old mansion," I said.

He frowned at me. "You've been in my laboratories? How did you find them? Who told you of where they were hidden?"

"I sorta bashed a huge fuckin' hole in your kitchen floor and fell into one of them. Found a dead American soldier — Charlie. You know about him?"

Horst's next grin was one filled with such malice that I swore I was sitting across from Satan himself. "Oh, yes. He and his little group were the first to find my experiments." He chuckled, dry and pained. "And the last."

"What did you do to them?" Gus asked nervously.

Eyes like bits of fiery coal flicked towards him.

"I took weak soldiers," Horst rasped, "and I made them *strong*."

My mouth tightened; something clicked.

The underground lab. The chair in the tower, directly underneath a hole in the ceiling. The mutated spook, ferocious and bestial, yet desperate for death when clarity could break through its implanted urges.

Charlie, imprisoned and howling in regret, being ripped from this realm as he found a blackened skeleton. His subordinate's. His friend's. His failure, plain in front of eyes in the form of ashen bones and ruined skulls.

"*They* were your super-soldiers," I said. "Charlie's squad. You beefed them up, made them inhumanly strong. How?"

"The power of God," Horst said, throwing his head back and opening his arms as if inviting an embrace from the heavens.

"And how...Why did they follow your orders?" Gus asked.

Horst pointed to his temple, nodding his head shakily and grinning.

"The metal plate. You were tapped into them. Fucking with their heads."

"Yes," he wheezed. "They went where I wanted, when I wanted, did what I wanted — veritable deities in the palm of the Reich's hand."

"So," I said after a minute, "what happened? Why didn't those things make it to the front lines?"

Erick's expression dropped into one of anger. Disappointment. Even shame. "In my hubris, I was discovered. I should never have captured that boy — the soldier you called Charlie. I assumed I was above the law, that the Americans would never catch me, but that boy's disappearance was all the proof they needed to warrant a raid of my estate." He clenched his jaw, shaking in anger. "That was their only flaw: Anyone with the proper knowledge could sway the soldiers. Said knowledge could be found in many places within my laboratories, so I..." An honest to God tear fell down the Nazi's face. "I had to kill them — my creations, my children — lest they fell into the hands of the Americans. I let the Reich down... I let *her* down. Their mission went unaccomplished, and that I shall regret until the day I die."

That's it. That's why Beefman's spook was so aggressive, yet so willing to pass on when I'd attacked back. It had a mission — a duty so deeply implanted into its psyche it carried over into his afterlife. They couldn't move on, not while there were still Americans to kill and a duty to fulfill. Not until they'd given it an honest try, at least. That explained the corrupted spook; it was *programmed* to live, to search, to kill. It left the haunt not because it wanted to, but because it was told to.

"How many were there?" Gus asked.

"23," Horst replied, throat tight.

Gus gasped through his teeth and looked at me.

"23 Nazi Zombie Super Soldier Ghost Frankenstein's Monsters," I said. "Fucking awesome."

There was a silence as that idea lingered — Gus terrified, Horst's emotions melting into exhaustion and confusion. Gus looked like he wanted to ask further questions, but the old man was practically dying in front of us.

"Well, um, thanks for talking with us, I guess. We'll just leave you—"

"Why don't you go ahead, Gus," I said, staring at Horst. "There are a few more things I'd like to bounce off this old coot."

"Really? You don't think we should get back to thc mansion as soon as possible?"

"Oh, this won't take long." I grinned.

Gus had nothing to say to that, so he left silently, ignored by both of us.

I leaned back and crossed my legs, lacing my fingers over my lap. "So, Erick." Horst's tired eyes were working hard to remain focused, but he looked at me eventually. "Let's chat."

Chapter 16

Code of Conduct

What... do you want...?" Made obvious by his desperate struggle with his own lungs, Horst's time was running short. Well, his miserable life was about to receive an even *more* miserable extension.

"Tell me, Erick," I said. "How many people do you think you've killed? Ballpark figures are fine."

He scoffed. "Every death was in the name of—"

"Just humor me, you old creep."

Horst eyed me, then sat in thought for a moment. "With the lives that my information may have put in danger, and those killed by my own hand during experiments... hundreds of thousands." His breaths came out a little less forced as he puffed out his chest with pride.

"Not bad, not bad," I said, nodding. "And I assume you don't feel the slightest remorse for any of those?"

"Of course not," he spat. "Each of them were scum. Lesser beings that—"

"Perfect! Well, Mr. Horst, everything in your resume looks great. You got the job!"

Light erupted in a halo of white as I drew Baby, the choir announcing her holy appearance. Horst took a ragged breath and flinched away, immediately panicked at the appearance of the deadly Blade. I showed my teeth to him.

"Oh, she ain't for you, buddy boy. You've got something

much, *much* worse coming up." Carefully, I placed my index finger on the point of Baby's blade. I lightly ran my finger down her entire length. Blood, surrounded by a dim white glow, trickled down my hand, droplets tarnishing Baby's radiance. I reached her hilt and pulled my finger away. "Sorry, girl," I whispered, wiping away the red and sheathing her.

I knelt and painted a symbol with my blood: A circle with one line jutting upwards from its center, then two squiggles streaming from the tip of that line and encircling the entire shape; Agatha's summoning symbol. I stood and looked at the drawing as light radiated from the red lines, waiting for her to arrive.

A soft whooshing — along with a ten-degree drop in temperature — and the demi-goddess was there, staring down at me in all her resplendence.

"Graves," Agatha said, her voice echoing surreally through the brick room. Horst's eyes opened wide. The Nazi gripped the armrests, jowls jiggling. I hoped the old bastard didn't fart out on me now, just from seeing an otherworldly semi-deity.

"I found you a host, bitch," I said, putting my hands on my hips and grinning in triumph.

She eyed me questioningly and I gestured towards Erick, whose expression had melted into one of pure... joy? Tears pooled in his eyes as he stared at Agatha, a trembling smile creeping across his wrinkled, drooping face.

"You cannot be serious," she said, ignoring him. "This is an old man. Pathetic. Harmless."

"Ah, yes — *now* he is. But this isn't your average pathetic piece of shit, this is *the* Erick Horst!" I did my best impersonation of a game show host, gesticulating wildly. "Nazi, mad scientist, murderer extraordinaire!"

Agatha was unamused, but she floated over and inspected Erick — who mumbled under his breath in rhythmic diction, as if he were repeating a joyful prayer. "You are telling me that this man directly participated in the... What is that genocide called? The 'Holocaust'?"

"That is correct, you gaseous wench. Say what you will about *me*, but I sure as shit didn't sit by and watch my nation slaughter millions."

"I suppose that is true," Agatha said, folding her arms. "But this host is unfit for my form. I worry that he will fall apart the minute I possess him."

"Not my problem, you buoyant bimbo. You know the deal: The Big Guy forgives whatever souls-debt I owe if *you* get a host — one that's got 'a more wicked heart than mine.' You can *try* to Monkey's Paw your way out of this one, bitch, but you can't get more objectively evil than a Nazi!" I did a little dance in place, clicking my heels.

Agatha stared at me with no expression, then returned to studying Horst. She seemed conflicted; she couldn't go against her boss, so she had no choice but to accept this Host and be done with the whole ordeal — but man, did she ever hate letting me win! I'd finally be free from all of the Other Side's prejudice. Baby would be secure in possession, once and for all — mine to do with what I please. I could continue my quest.

Revenge never felt so *close*.

I chuckled to myself as Agatha focused on Horst, his breath picking up rapidly. Sweat beaded on his forehead. His eyes rolled back. The Nazi recognized something was wrong, that Agatha was about to—

Horst's head fell off.

Just fell right the fuck off. Into his lap like a freshly picked watermelon. No blood, no noise, nothing. Just a clean cut and a dry wound. His sliced esophagus was still squirming, desperate for breath. Even his spinal cord had been cut through like a piece of sushi. Erick's severed head sat on his legs, staring at me with that same tired, vacant expression, his decades of silent torment finally over.

"Mmm," Agatha mewed behind me. "Pity."

My mouth clicked as I picked my jaw up from the floor. "That is fucking cheating."

"Oh, please," Agatha said, giggling. "Have you *still* not realized how inevitable it is, Graves? Your death, I mean. *You* decided to leave us. *You* decided to remain mortal. Now you blame *me* when your time comes? You could have had *no* 'time,' Graves. No limit to your span of life. Now..." she clucked her teeth and shook her head, "you die. Just like the rest of your mortal kin. And Chronalius will finally move on to someone more worthy."

The sleeves and dress on Agatha's flowing gown dissipated like powder, turning into mist and forming an elongated shape in her right hand. Both Agatha and the shape gave off a light nearly bright enough to melt eyes from their sockets like wax. That brightness subsided, revealing Agatha in a short battle skirt and a leather vest, studded with metal and plated in bits of gold. She held a radiant broadsword expertly at her side.

"None of us know what happens when our souls are Severed from the Other Side. Not even the Reaper." She smiled. "Where is there to go after the final resting place? Some say rebirth. Some say another layer of afterlife." Half of Agatha's face melted like before, revealing that purple skull, teeth like a bear's, and eyes so sharp I had to look away. The skin dripped from her chin and pooled on the brick floor, steaming. "But I have my own theory, Bastard," she said, voice now gravely and monstrous. "I think there is nothing beyond. Blackness. Your consciousness would fade like a memory, lost in the halls of time and forgotten."

She doubled over, hands tight on her sword's grip, ready to kill me in one move.

"Oh won't you tell me, Graves!?" Agatha cackled. *"After I send you there, if your mind does not dissipate like sand in water, won't you come and tell me what to expect!?"*

Her laugh was like a shriek, slapping the walls and bouncing around the room. Agatha seemed to have her own, constant death hum — a shrill sound like nails in a blender. Her laughter cut off abruptly as she blasted forward, coming to remove my head.

And she was stopped.

Before I could even consider fighting back, before I had a chance to draw Baby or my shotgun — to prepare in any way — a wall of blackness spread out in front of me. It squirmed and writhed as if it were living, tendrils of shadow randomly whipping out from its exterior. Agatha stopped before it spread completely, face quickly reverting to her neutral beauty, an instinctual reaction to surprise.

The wall sat between us for a moment, undulating like the surface of the ocean. I stared into the stretch of blackness, mystified, Agatha's form distorted and darkened as it was filtered through the force. After a dense silence, it reverted into itself and formed into a black sphere, about the size of a basketball.

Agatha was on her knees, head bowed, hands laced together in a sort of prayer. She was mumbling under her breath. Pleading. Begging.

"I meant no insult, Lord," she whispered quickly. "I went against your wishes, but I did so unknowingly. Fury masked my other senses, great Reaper, otherwise I never would have *thought* to disobey you." Her pleading stopped; her screeching hum waned. Deafening silence followed. The sphere of shadow still floated, unsatisfied. Agatha looked at it, almost *panicked.* I'd never seen her that way.

Slowly, Agatha's pristine features fell; her head sagged, as if she were resigned to some fate. She brought up a limp, pale arm, offering it to the ball of shadow. The orb quickly *swished* forward, encasing everything up to the elbow, its utter black in contrast to the demi-goddess' pearly white skin. Agatha was expressionless, but her shoulders trembled.

Eventually, the orb slowly moved away from her arm. Seemingly content, it sucked into itself.

It left Agatha's arm completely, wholly, black. No visible bones, or veins, or even fingernails. Like it was silhouetted behind a curtain. I smiled.

She was Marked. That was strike one; one more and she'd be... *out,* if you get me. The Reaper may not care much for mortal existence, but rules are rules. I watched her — staring at her black limb and nearly sobbing — then threw back my head and roared in laughter.

"HA!" I bellowed. "Looks like the big bad Reaper has a code of conduct after all!" I pointed towards the ground and fingerbanged. "Good lookin' out, you crotchety old dickhead!"

Agatha shot me with a wicked glare, but I gave her a wide smile in return.

"Methinks I've got some more time, bitch. Why don't you go polish your dumb *normal* sword while you wait?"

Light enveloped her body as she floated from the floor. She looked down at me and said, "Midnight tonight is when you breathe your last."

I put my middle finger up and turned to leave before she could. Agatha growled when I did, but left all the same, bright light flashing.

Boo-ya! Graves averts Death once again, baby! Easy peasy!

Now I just had to return to Jennifer's mansion, defeat an army of Nazi super-soldier ghosts, pay off Josephi, and track down someone who's done more awful shit than I have to retain my mortal soul and prevent a demi-goddess of death from taking my ancient, magical blade. All before midnight.

Lemon flippin' squeezy!

"Did... Is Horst dead?" the guard asked, side-eyeing me as I left the room.

Fuck. "Uh, no, he's just... sleeping."

The guard stood in front of me and peered into the room — at Erick Horst's severed head and cooling corpse — then nodded knowingly. He stepped out of my way.

It wasn't until then that I realized the guards had let a fully armed man into a private room with a prisoner — that's not protocol, I wouldn't think. *I guess Horst was hated by more than the US government.* A chill went through me.

Note to self: Don't be a Nazi.

The rain had picked up; even filtered through the trees, it covered my skin in a thin sheen. Gus dozed in the van, feet propped up on the dash. He flinched awake as I closed the passenger door. "What took you?" he yawned, rubbing the sleep out of his eyes.

"Horst was surprisingly talkative. I must have a little Aryan in me or something."

I caught the faintest hint of an eyeroll, but Gus didn't push the subject. *He's learning.*

"So, what's next?" he asked as we drove through the forest. The sunlight was dimming, and the deep darkness between the trees was becoming deeper and darker.

Tik-tok, tik-tok.

"I have to take care of those ghosts at Jenny's mansion...

which ain't gonna be easy. I mean, 23 is nothing to sneeze at — even if we've already taken down two. The frankenspooks are some of the tougher things I've faced, and they're clearly resilient; cuts and slices aren't gonna be enough. When I go against these things, I'm gonna need to be *precise*." I was mostly talking to myself, rationalizing and collecting my thoughts.

"What can I do to help?"

"You can drop me off, then head home. Your usefulness here is about dried up."

"What... what do you mean?" he asked quietly.

"I mean that I don't need gadgets, or wheels, or Watsons. I've got my sword and my shotty. Those spooks will have enough of an advantage without you getting in my way. My balls are on the line here; wouldn't do if you were trodding all over them."

Gus wilted, eyes hard on the splashing road, but said, "How on Earth do you plan on Severing all of those things on your own?"

I shrugged. "I'm not sure, Gus, but I know that you wouldn't be able to help."

"But, the Specterencasing Cuboid—"

"Ain't gonna do shit when *21* of those fuckers come for me," I said firmly. "You're not even getting paid here. Why the fuck do you care?"

Gus frowned, his watery eyes focused and suddenly determined, contemplative.

"Their only flaw..." he mumbled to himself after a few minutes.

"What was that?"

He didn't reply, submerged in his inner monologue. The rest of the ride went like that.

I let the phone's voice do the actual direction-ing while I stared at the dreary, wet scenery and pondered my impending doom.

Chapter 17

Honed Skills

By the time we puttered back up to Jennifer's mansion, it was nearly dark. Heavy rain pattered on the van's windshield, already forming puddles on the asphalt and turning the grassy hill into more of a squishing swamp.

"When do you think you'll do it?" Gus asked, turning off the ignition.

"Let's just say I'm on sort of a strict time limit. I'll need to get their attention and wipe them out as soon as possible. Then I've got a date with the devil." He eyed me. "By that, I mean Josephi."

"Ah." His eyes were glued to the haunt, moving up and down its length as if it were a Christmas gift just waiting to be unwrapped. "Got any hunches?"

"Horst himself said that his 'soldiers' had been killed in the same way they were created, so I'll have to go wherever both of those things happened."

"And where is that?"

"There's one lab in the basement filled with a bunch of weird, glass tubes that I'm sure had something to do with... something."

"'Weird glass tubes,' huh? That definitely sounds interesting."

"Yeah," I said, narrowing my eyes at him. "Then there's the lab where we took down Beefman— er, the first frankenspook. The room with the perfectly lightning-sized hole in the ceiling, and chair on a pole with a big lever next to it, directly under said lightning-sized hole. Call me crazy, but I'd say that these things were being shocked to life or some shit. Maybe I've just seen too many movies."

"'The power of God,'" Gus quoted.

"Yup. If there's one thing the Big G's good at it's whipping up monsters."

The medium was clearly in a ponderous mood, as he sat back in the driver's seat and squinted at the tip of the right tower, with the lab at its top.

"So," he said, not looking away, "which lab first?"

"Both of them have a death hum, but I found a set of fucked up bones in the underground one, so I figure that's my safest bet. There wasn't much time for me to look around while I was down there."

"Perfect." Gus' chubby cheeks dimpled with his smile.

"Yeah. I'm gonna try and make some noise and kick some shit around until... What do you mean 'perfect'?"

"I meant that it's good you're going to the underground lab, because *I* want to further investigate the one inside the tower."

I rolled my eyes. "Kid, I already told you. You'll only—"

"This is as much my case as yours, Graves. I have a right to pursue any leads that come to my mind."

The guy still didn't look at me; he was so focused on his thoughts he didn't realize he should've feared confronting me.

The fact was that I *couldn't* let him interfere. If he fucked something up, not only would 21 frankenspooks be left to tear through Hartsville like a whacker through weeds, but I wouldn't get paid, so I wouldn't be able to pay Josephi, so I'd get booted from the Union.

I'd also fucking die, and Agatha would be unleashed upon the mortal realm with Baby and plenty of souls to reap.

But...

Gus had proven himself competent. He'd shown that he could be resourceful and cunning. That his unique set of skills were completely out of my realm of understanding. Shit, if Gus hadn't been there when I'd confronted Beefman, I'd be fucking dead already.

He stared at the mansion with complete determination, ready to tackle the challenge and come out ahead — it seemed the kid still had something to prove to the other Detectors, especially Jessie, his lost love. Who was I to stop the poor sap? He could knock himself out.

"Alright, don't say I didn't fucking warn you." I popped open the door and left to go investigate the underground laboratory.

Thankfully, I didn't have to fall dozens of feet while clinging to a six-foot, naked beefcake to get there this time.

The trap door wasn't as heavy as I remembered — probably because I wasn't lugging a 400-pound rhinoceros — and it pulled open smoothly. The stench of dust and death met me as I climbed down the spiraling stairs.

Fluorescent lights buzzed like bugs, joining with the hum to create an atmosphere that made me want to check my boxers for spiders. Dust settled comfortably on each surface; not so much as a breeze stirred it. The tube that held the charred remains was still left open. I crouched cautiously and picked up the warped skull.

The skull — its jagged or missing teeth, fractured nose, uneven shape, the various lumps of added bone — matched the frankenspooks' appearance to a T.

The metal plate drilled into the thing's temple gleamed

after I wiped the dust from it. German language was engraved onto its center, which I couldn't read. I *could* read the triangular warning symbol, encased by little lightning bolts. To me, that read *high voltage*.

Enough stalling. It was time to move onto something I've always been great at:

Making a big ol' ruckus.

I faced a metal table, covered in expcnsivc-looking medical equipment and glassware, then kicked it over. Glass shattered; metal clanged raucously. The table fell apart, clattering against everything in sight, eventually coming to a dusty rest after grinding against the concrete for a few feet.

The hum ticked up, becoming more growl than groan.

I picked up a few pieces of dented metal and banged them together, like a monkey would his cymbals. "Wakey, wakey, you fucking freaks! Eggs and bakey over here! First come, first served!" The groan got a little louder.

I took a big inhale, held my hands in front of my mouth like I was holding a trumpet, then did my best vocal rendition of the Military Bugle Wake Up Call until my lungs were empty. Still louder, a constant droning grumble, a contemplating predator.

"Yeah, yeah! There's a fresh, supple American over here!" I shouted, losing breath. "Barbeques! Blonde with big swingin' milkers, stuffed into skin-tight bikinis! Equal rights!"

That did it; a snatch of the hum broke away, like a piece of cotton candy ripped from the rest, and focused directly to my right. One of the frankenspooks had come to play, thinking himself still invisible and untraceable, and thinking me an easy, vulnerable prey.

Sorry for him, this prey had claws.

Baby's radiance pushed back the fluorescent lighting, a

battle of beams. With her brightness, the frankenspook was revealed, too close for comfort. It was a little different than the first two guys, but he was definitely one of Horst's soldiers. One of Charlie's squad mates.

"There you go, you big lug," I said, facing him. Despite his growls, and the blasting hum, the frankenspook still seemed dormant; his face didn't contort in anger, nor did he gnash his ruined teeth with ferocious hunger. "Just stay calm. The H-man won. There's nothing to worry about." The frankenspook shied away from Baby's light, whimpering like a beaten puppy. I shushed him. "There, there. Time to rest."

With a quick movement, I stabbed Baby into his bulbous neck. Fear left his eye, and his whimpering stopped. He stiffened.

Then he screamed.

You ever hear a wildcat roar? It's a shrill sort of noise, almost like a woman's scream but shorter, sharper. Those roars single-handedly spawned *dozens* of folktales. They sound so human, yet they had no discernable origin. When the screams break through the quiet of a midnight forest, campers jump to the easiest conclusion: An innocent woman was just murdered in the dead of night, shrieking in anguish and panic, and *they're* next. It's the sorta noise that pierces any semblance of rational thought that a human might have — reverts them back to the animal we each have caged inside us. The one desperate to run. To escape. To survive.

The super soldier's scream was like that but a billion times louder, longer, and right fucking next to me.

It shook the ground like an earthquake, beakers clinking, metal clanging, my teeth clacking. As it droned on, it lost all meaning. It wasn't a scream of pain or fear, it was mechanical. A tool that had been left on. I couldn't think about what that tool was being used for.

Because I was too busy swearing to Christ that I'd never hear anything again.

I screamed right alongside the frankenspook, holding my ears and rocking my head. Baby clanged to the floor, her light dimmed.

Then it stopped. Shut off as suddenly as a stereo.

I sat there for a long time, my eyes shut tight and my head in my hands. To go from such an otherworldly loud sound to near absolute silence made me sicker than any gore I'd ever seen. I fell on my ass and gripped my stomach.

Finally, I slowly opened my eyes.

One, two, three, four, five, six — I swiveled my head around — seven, eight, nine, ten... yup. There were 20, alright.

Nearly two-fucking-dozen frankenspooks were in the lab. They looked around lethargically, seemingly devoid of thought. The one I'd stabbed had faded away, thankfully Severed. I don't know why it had screamed that way, but I guess it brought the rest of its pals out of standby. Which, all in all, could have been doing me a favor.

Feeling slightly optimistic, I reached over and grabbed Baby's hilt. She purred affectionately, her glow brightening. One of the spooks near me twitched a little, so I moved slowly. I pulled Baby over to me, grabbed her with both hands, then stood cautiously. I was hoping I could pick them off one-by-one, but that might change if this next frankenspook screamed like the previous one — a gamble, but it was all I had.

The spook did *not* scream as I plunged Baby into his stomach. He looked down at Baby, three feet deep in his guts, and grunted. His beady eyes followed her blade, her hilt, my arms, and ended on my face. Then he grunted again.

And swatted me away like a nipping mosquito.

I flew backwards, Baby still in my grip, and crashed into a metal table. The noise was about as resounding as any unequipped human being can make; glassware rattled on top of the table, some fell and shattered into tinkling shards. As I sat there, dazed, I realized a few things.

One, beheading was the only attack that would fatally wound these things. While that frankenspook *should* have been immediately Severed from Baby churning so deep in his insides, he'd shrugged it off. In fact, he was already in tip-top shape and stumbling towards me.

Which brings me to number two: All 20 of the fuckers were looking right at me. They didn't seem angry or frightened or surprised. They looked hungry. I was like a big Christmas ham right around then, grease and stuffing steaming in the winter's chill, flesh as tender and salty as could be expected.

It ain't easy to cut something's head off. Even if that thing's standing totally still, even if the weapon is designed to slice through them like scissors through tape, the precision and steadiness it takes to behead proficiently requires *years* of mastery, and practically inhuman strength.

Now, imagine doing that to a *moving* target. While you're at it, imagine *20* moving fuckin' targets.

Things weren't looking that great.

With a growl, the frankenspook I'd stabbed lunged for me. I sidestepped, but rammed right into another one I hadn't even seen. I expected the thing to break my neck, but it pushed me forward and into the crowd. They weren't gonna let me pick them off.

The fucking monsters were better at planning than *I* was.

Arms wrapped all around me, thick as ancient roots. They seemed to caress for a bit as I struggled, like they were trying to find the most fatal place to squeeze until it popped. Then they started ripping.

I screamed and raised my sword. I desperately swung her around me, trying to knick at least one of my captors. They dodged easily. Effortlessly.

Their gnarled, bloody, mutilated paws darted in and out like dozens of little knives, pinching and cutting and pulling. One of the frankenspooks wrapped a thick arm around my neck, breaking off all oxygen. My vision faded, my struggles weakened. I ran out strength... and breath... I—

Baby *exploded* with light.

Every inch of my sight was made pure white. Every object in the lab, every wall, filled with unmitigated brightness. The spooks reeled and screamed in response, until they too were absorbed in the glow. I fell right back on my ass, Baby rumbling hungrily in my hand.

Which was still there.

The light had consumed everything except *me*. I was sitting in a bleach-white field, nothing standing out or signifying distance. It was blinding and mesmerizing at once. Baby struggled in my grasp.

"Easy girl!" I yelled. She buzzed and squealed like iron under a fire, then the light was *sucked* back into her. It didn't just dim, or blink out, the light physically *retracted* from our surroundings and returned to Baby. She'd never done that before. I have no idea what triggered it, but it didn't seem like a defense mechanism. More like testing her prey — a prodding, and an announcement of her strength.

And, while it was impressive and all, it really didn't do shit.

The spooks were still there. Dazed, true, but still Nazi monster ghosts. They wiped at their eyes like wounded cats, whimpering and growling and screaming. Some of them whipped their heads around, clearly blinded and trying to get a grasp on their surroundings.

I realized that Baby had given me an opportunity to show off another technique that I've mastered over the years:

I skedaddled. Retreated. Got the fuck outta there.

I ran towards the bottom of the spiraling staircase, towards the bookcase.

Ten of the frankenspooks blocked the exit, each bumping into one another like blind mice. "You little bitches," I hissed, rapidly searching for another escape route. The hairs on my neck stood as a few others stumbled closer to me. I pivoted on my heel and ran towards the other end of the lab — towards the holding cells.

Light retreated as I sprinted deeper into the dark stone halls. The frankenspooks' growls faded too; the only noises were the dimmed hum and thunder grumbling far, far above me, through hundreds of feet of earth.

My footsteps skidded as I slowed to a stop. A dead end. I rubbernecked and tried to gather my surroundings.

Shadows. A tiny prick of light streamed from the lab, what seemed miles away. I turned on my wrist-light and shined it around the dusty halls and met just that: Dust, and a whole lot of it. Cells marked the wall all along its length, empty save for bugs and dirt, their bars rusted red.

A bizarrely asymmetrical opening yawned to my right. It arched, one side somewhat smooth, the other more like rough stone. There was a definite supernatural energy coming from inside it... but that wasn't a death hum. It was high-pitched and singing. A siren's song.

With nowhere else to turn, and a horde of frankenspooks on my tail, I had the chance to show of the third of my three skills: being a fucking moron.

I walked through the jagged cave mouth and into the shadow-drenched unknown.

Chapter 18

Threads

Because of its jagged, weirdly shaped opening, I expected this passage's innards to be less... organized. But no, if anything it was *more* put together than the rest of the mansion. It was also decidedly more medieval.

The concrete walls had gradually given way to solid blocks of brick, much larger than the ones we saw leading into the upper laboratory. This material was colored a dulled burgundy, speckled with brighter red revealed by the brick's chipped surface. Instead of being square like the other hallways and tunnels within the mansion, this one's ceiling was rounded, forming an arch. Square, fist-sized openings routinely appeared on either wall, sometimes with a burnt torch slipped into them, stringed with cobwebs.

I walked for a long time, the rumbling thunder and scratchy footsteps my only company, until I spotted any difference in the environment: A faded symbol, painted on the wall with a dried brown substance. It had been rubbed away to the point of being illegible — but still, it felt... familiar. As I continued walking, I spotted four more of the drawings, each vaguely round and surrounded by lines but otherwise patternless.

Eventually, I reached the end of the hallway, walking below another arch.

And into a garden. Hundreds of feet beneath the surface of

the Earth.

A wilted, pathetic tree sprouted in its center, surrounded by dusty, hard soil. An oblong statue jutted out from the ground, indiscernible from where I was standing. Stubborn stems cracked like tinder as I walked over a shallow, dried pit that curved randomly around the room — what must have once held a small river. It was disorienting to see something meant to bathed in sunlight submerged in such complete darkness. *How the fuck is there a tree* at all*?* I thought, studying the surprisingly low ceiling.

Without wind to buffer it over the decades, the statue was perfectly symmetrical, but it wasn't really remarkable... save for something carved into its front. I crept closer to the statue and squinted, trying to make out the carving.

It was a simple shape: a circle with one straight line stemming from its center. Two wavy lines streamed from the tip of that line and encircled the entire carving.

Agatha's summoning symbol.

"What the fucking fuck..." I whispered, circling the statue.

I jumped when I saw its face — or *faces*.

The entire statue was split in half, right down the middle. One half had Agatha's beautiful face. Her eye was closed, her plush lips curved in a friendly yet cunning smile. A stone rendition of her hair flowed over her shoulder. Similarly, her gown was depicted as wavy, despite being completely still. Her body was as curved as it was in life, but her hair surrounded it, thus making both halves symmetrical when viewed from the back.

The other half was of her more hostile personality. Her chiseled skull was exposed, jagged teeth jutting out somehow cleanly, her canines pointy and long. And that eye... it was as unnerving as if she were there in the "flesh." It was perfectly rounded — emotionless, bestial — with a tiny, focused pupil, somehow conveying fury and hunger at once. In this half's clawed, veined hand was Agatha's broadsword, pointed towards the soil.

I moved closer to the statue, thoughts and theories zipping through my head. *Why the hell is there a shrine to Agatha in Horst's basement?* People of this realm worship gods and demi-gods all the time, true, but Agatha really wasn't anything special. She wasn't "the goddess of titties" or anything, just your average minor deity. She always *wanted* to be more, to have power both physically in the form of Baby and politically within the Other Side, but she'd been denied each time she tried to seize any.

Was she working *with Horst? Why would—*

My foot moved downwards, pressing in a large switch that thudded against the stone below it after shifting a few inches. The ground below me shook slightly, then it spun slowly, the statue with it. After it spun about 180 degrees, it snapped into place and rose from the earth. Now that it was elevated, I saw that the platform was around six feet in circumference.

As I neared the ceiling, a round hole slid open directly above the platform. I moved into the opening with little room to spare, but the stone elevator didn't stop. My wristlight showed solid walls surrounding me, not an exit in sight. The sounds of rain slapping and thunder rumbling neared, accented by brick grinding on brick. I should probably have been more cautious — for all I knew, this could have been a trap meant to squish me against a second ceiling — but I was too confused and disoriented by the possibilities that Agatha's shrine brought to this case.

Eventually, a second hole ground open, letting in dim light that seemed bright by contrast with the darkness I was trapped in. I was squinting and rubbing my eyes, adjusting to the natural light, when someone yelped pathetically near me.

There was a thud as they fell, and a satisfying *click* when the platform finally stopped rising.

The entire room was much more lit than the last time we'd been here, despite the minimal light streaming through the hole in the ceiling. Rain, however, *did* come through the hole, slapping against the platform above us.

"Graves!?" Gus yelled. "What... Where the *heck* did you come from!?"

"I have no fucking clue," I mumbled. "But what I saw there did not bode well." I reached down and pulled him up, grunting.

"What is *that*?" Gus asked, noticing the statue.

"Some ugly lady that Horst had a boner for, I guess."

Hours in my presence must have really fine-tuned Gus' bullshit-adar because he frowned at me without saying anything.

I quickly changed the subject. "You find anything up here?"

"Horst's journals," he replied, picking some papers up.

"Anything good? Or the same old Nazi shit?"

"Mostly theories and hypothesis concerning the creation of his soldiers... and Nazi stuff," Gus replied, musing. "Horst would first kill, then mutate his specimens, giving them strength beyond that of any regular person. Then, he'd strap their carcass to that chair and send them up through the tower's roof, which is the highest point reachable for dozens of miles around. We were right; he used lightning to reanimate them." The medium scratched his head, looking confused but intently curious. "Although... Horst never goes into detail about the actual *means* of mutation — what he actually *did* to make them so inhumanly strong — nor does he elaborate on the precise method of reanimation. I mean... it can't *all* be from the lightning, right?"

I said nothing, but theories buzzed around my skull.

"Also," Gus continued, "Erick continuously brings up a *second* benefactor, other than the German military and Nazi party. He writes very vaguely about them, but he seems to have really respected them. Like, *really* respected them.

"Listen to this: 'My dearest light, my midnight pearl, what more can I do? You have given me power, so I will give you *death*. The death that you are so desperate for, for which you all but pleaded. They will kill *millions*, my pearl, and maybe that will earn you what you have lusted after. And the item that you believe each severed soul will fuel, I will never forget. It is important to you, so it is *crucial* to me. So, so, crucial...'"

"Jesus," I said. "When Horst gets a stiffy, he doesn't beat around the bush."

"Whoever this was was someone *big*, Graves. Look, this is written in *Latin*." Gus flashed the paper. Lovely, meticulously scrawled words waved on each line. Latin is the preferred language for many members of the afterlife, so many in the Union were fluent. "I think that means he didn't want his comrades discovering this other benefactor. I doubt it was the US, but it had to be someone with power. Enough power to bring the dead back to life..."

This was getting fucked up. Too many loose ends — which seemingly had nothing to do with one another — were being stringed together. Agatha and Horst, the frankenspooks and the politics within the Other Side. But there was still something missing…

"This is it!" he said.

"The traitor's secret source?" I asked cautiously. I wasn't sure why, but some part of me didn't want Gus to get involved with Agatha, or the Other Side in general.

"No, it's their weakness. Their only flaw! Here, he writes,

'The soldiers are strong but weak at once. They may have power to kill and maim, but it is not difficult to take control of them. One needs only to know the correct word to manipulate the neuro-plates attached to their prefrontal cortex. Only I know their word, and I plan to take it to my grave.'"

"Shit," I mumbled.

"What do you mean? This is pcrfcct! If the motives ingrained in their plates are still active even after they've died, why wouldn't this be the same? We can drive back to Haggard Prison and pry the deactivation phrase out of Horst's mouth!"

"It's not that it won't work, kid. It's that Horst *did* take it to his grave."

"*What!?*" Gus yelled.

Lightning struck, suddenly brightening the laboratory, revealing its towering height.

"What do you mean?" Gus demanded, hardly off-put by the sudden flash. "What aren't you telling—"

Thunder *cracked* like an explosion of TNT, reverberating through the lab as if we were in a giant ringing bell. The rumble that followed was ominous. Impatient. Hungry.

"I mean that the old fart croaked!" I yelled.

"How? We *just* spoke with him!" He grinded his teeth. "What did you do?"

"It's a long fuckin' story that I don't particularly feel like getting into right now — don't fucking push it, Gus."

The medium's mouth snapped close as he sneered, but he took a breath and calmed himself. "Fine. He's dead. We'll have to figure out the deactivation word ourselves."

"Let's be quick about it," I said over the pounding rain. "I, uh, *woke up* the spooks while I was underground. My sword disoriented them, but I have no clue how long that'll last."

"T-they're *awake*?" His teeth practically chattered. "Did you m-manage to Sever any?"

"Yeah. One."

"*One!?* So there are 20 super-soldiers coming after us right now!?"

"Yes," I replied, looking up at the ceiling, which randomly flashed in time with the lightning. "My sword isn't very good at killing them — I figure it's got something to do with how anchored their motives are to this realm — so I think I'm gonna *need* Horst's word."

Gus' chest rose and fell quickly. His eyes darted around the room, desperate for an exit. An escape. Some way to retreat from the monsters out to rip him limb from limb, to mash his head in, to make sure that he never saw Jessie again.

I turned and gripped his shoulder. Rain and lightning still danced above us.

"Kid," I said, glaring into his eyes, "you knew what you were getting into when you came in here. You managed to find something useful, now just keep it up." He tried to look away, but I slapped him on the side of the head. "Stay focused. You've made it this far. I'm willing to bet that those fuckers will come right towards us now that they're awake. This tower is like a fuckin' megaphone for the thunder — a beacon of lightning to those cocksuckers.

"When they get here, *I'm* gonna distract them. I've got my sword and shotty, and plenty of defense. But mine isn't the most important job. While I'm fighting those ugly idiots off, *you* need to hunt through Horst's journal entries and find me that damn word. Do you hear me?"

"I..." Gus whimpered.

"I said, *do you fucking hear me!?*"

"I do... I do, Graves."

"Damn fuckin' straight, you do," I said, grinning and

patting him on the shoulder.

He took a deep breath, smiled shakily back, then ran towards the table and rifled through the stacks of papers.

I sat on the ground, bending my knees and tucking my feet into the crooks of my legs, while crossing my arms and shutting my eyes gently. I hoped I had enough time to meditate.

Yes, I said meditatc. No, I'm not a complete pussy.

It fucking works, alright?

I inhaled slowly through my nose, let my heartbeat five times, then breathed out in time with the next five beats. My lungs were left empty until the next batch of thunder rumbled above me. I sucked in cold air through my mouth, held it, breathed it through my nostrils, then did the reverse.

The grainy scent of moisture on wood rushed into my senses. The pattering of rain seemed to undulate alongside my heart's thumping. Even with my eyes closed, lightning lit up my vision. It filtered through my eyelids and became a warm red color, squiggling veins silhouetted like dormant worms. Thunder growled, deep and sharp, then faded in an exhale of grumbles; the Earth was snoring.

Then came the moans. The pig-like squeals and screams.

They'd come for us.

Let's fucking do this.

Chapter 19

Item of Power

Baby's smooth leather, gripped tightly in my fist, was a small comfort — as was her pulsating light, almost mechanical in its rhythm, like a car's brake lights.

Four, five, six, seven frankenspooks seeped from the floor like fog. They weren't dazed or confused or stupid; they each swiveled towards me as they came into the room. Again, the monsters didn't float towards me one-by-one, they moved like a wave, each spook a precise distance from another, prepared to patiently overwhelm me. I held Baby forward, periodically keeping an eye on Gus to make sure that he wasn't ambushed. I waved her back and forth, trying to ward the spooks off. But they simply stared at her, seemingly mesmerized but undeterred.

Baby pierced the chest of the spook nearest to me as I quickly jabbed her forward. The monster flinched back, pulling off her blade, then continued floating as its wound healed over. *Well, I can at least fend them off... sorta.*

Gus yelped behind me. I turned to look, but a spook made a sudden leap for my legs. He was most likely trying to pin me down so I couldn't retreat, but I jumped just in time and he landed right under me. I'd started twisting Baby before I even left the ground, so I finished the turn and fell back onto the spook with the blade pointed downward. Baby slammed through his neck and into the floor. I leveraged her grip, pulling towards me and away from the spook's body, and pried his head off like a bottle cap, glowing blood bursting.

One down, I thought as I spun Baby around to ward off any of the monsters that might take advantage of my vulnerable position. Ectoplasm flung off of her blade.

Gus was still at work, rummaging through the crumpled papers. Spooks continued to appear next to him, but they each ignored him and floated straight for me.

Weird...

But don't look a Nazi Frankenstein's monster zombie super soldier ghost's gift horse in the mouth, I guess.

The crowd around me was about ten frankenspooks strong now. I swung my greatsword in the air, like a helicopter's blade, slicing and dicing frankenspooks in turn. But after I wounded one, another was always on the verge of attacking. I was a whirlwind of thrusts and swipes, just barely keeping the beasts at bay.

Then ten more showed up

They oozed naturally into the crowd. Neither they nor their cohorts acknowledged one another. These fuckin' things were of one mind, one body.

Three in front of me dove forward with claws aiming for my face. As I swung Baby horizontally with one arm, I reached and pulled out my shotty with the other. Baby sliced through each of the spooks' chests, the shotty sucked in a pair of shells greedily. Another soldier had been hiding behind those three. He took advantage of my vulnerable posture and made a jump for my feet...

But the pair of spooks behind me were much closer.

I tucked the shotgun in my opposite armpit, barrel facing behind me, while changing my footing so I could swing Baby vertically from this position. Gun and sword sang in delight as they struck. The shells did their job; I could hear the thumping as the two spooks, now semi-physical, collapsed and rolled along the floor. I sliced most of my frontal aggressor's neck, deep enough to Sever him. He fell with a sigh and instantly faded into blue mist.

Four more spooks came for me at once.

I can't do this.

Quickly, I cracked open and loaded my shotgun with two bulky black shells. I ducked under two of my aggressors — jabbing upwards and poking one of them in the gut — and shot the shells onto the ground. They rolled, glowing red, then stopped in place and pulsed rapidly. The heat from the shotgun had set off a timer inside of each shell, and I had about seven more seconds to tuck tail before they—

One of the spooks picked up a shell.

It looked at the bomb curiously for a moment — I swung Baby to my right, fighting off a spook who'd lunged for my arm — then turned its head and looked in my direction.

It lobbed the fucking shell at me.

I yelped, panicked, turning and running away from the careening bomb. I swung Baby like a weed whacker to carve a path forward. Blue blood sprayed, spectral flesh fell, but the spooks still stood. Just ahead of me sat the strange chair on its pole, it and the lever next to it soaked in rain. I burst through the crowd of spooks — some scratched my bare skin or ripped at my jumpsuit — and all-out sprinted towards the chair.

Right when I got to it, I heard the beeping of the grenade shell rapidly tick up in volume. Instinctively, I pivoted and swung Baby behind me, bracing for the worst.

The shell hit the flat of Baby's blade with a *clang*, and I swatted it away like a baseball. It arched, then fell back towards the crowd. It and its partner's beeping reached a crescendo at once, dull rims of red beating like an organ.

They exploded.

Granted, small as explosions go. But they still exploded.

Small spouts of fire and splintered wood erupted in the middle of the crowd. Thunder and fire roared together, until they both quieted. The explosions themselves wouldn't do much harm to the spooks unless they were attacking physically, but the light they gave off blinded them and forced them away.

The two unlucky fucks that I'd shot a bit ago were still somewhat rooted in this realm, however, so they got blasted to mother-loving smithereens.

While the crowd was distracted, I climbed onto the chair and peered at Gus. It looked like he had made his way through a lot of the papers, but he hadn't said anything yet. Not good. The spooks, still ignoring the medium, quickly reoriented themselves and moved towards me.

"Hey, buddy!" I yelled. "What's the deal? Find anything?"

"Not really!" Gus yelled in reply. "The guy just goes on and on about this third party! I wonder if they've got anything to do with the deactivation phrase!"

Now there's a thought...

A spook growled right next to me. I cleaved his skull. Another grabbed my foot, hanging just off the chair, so I shot him in the chest. I was surrounded — even if it was by a dozen spooks, it might as well have been an entire fucking ocean.

"Looks like Agatha ain't gonna get her chance to kill me," I mumbled, slicing and swiping randomly. Another spook howled on the other side of the chair. Aggressively, angrily, I swung Baby towards his neck. The attack was slower than it would have been an hour ago — fuck, a couple of *minutes* ago — and the monster ducked easily. My sword whizzed through the air, bringing my tired arms right along with it, then—

Clunk.

She hit something metallic and hollow. The chair I was squatting in shook, then moved upwards. I'd hit the lever.

I guess this is as good an escape route as any.

The chair was rising surprisingly quickly, my hair streaming in front of my eyes from the momentum and plastered to my forehead by the sudden force of the rain. Lightning flashed from the bright hole above me, like a portal to a different dimension, a home to some grumbling beast.

The spooks all looked up in unison, taken off-guard by my sudden flight but not necessarily surprised. They floated from the ground like freshly blown bubbles, hardly shifting in any other direction than up.

I braced myself, breathing with each shock of thunder, then corrected my stance so I'd be able to fire the shotty and slice with Baby in a 360-degree radius.

This was my final stand. If Gus couldn't get me the code, this was fuckin' it.

Rumble... inhale... *crash...* exhale... *rumble...* inhale—

Something grabbed my leg.

Without looking, I whipped around the shotty and blasted a spook in the face. He snarled as he fell away, semi-physical so somewhat adherent to the laws of gravity.

"I think I've got something!" Gus yelled. I looked over the levitating crowd around me — stabbing a frankenspook through the shoulder. Gus was standing at the base of the pole holding the chair, gripping a few soaked slips of paper.

"Spit it out, then!" I hollered back.

"Horst never wrote anything specific about the word, but he talks about one thing profusely! An item that his other benefactor was after! The name was unfamiliar to him, but he recited it over and in some sort of testament to his dedication!" He nervously studied the glowing crowd of monsters — and me, disheveled and exhausted. "It's the best we've got!"

The shotgun *popped* as I banged it on my other arm to open its chamber, two empty shells falling into the black abyss below me. I beheaded a spook with a quick swipe. Two shells — spread versions of the ones that ground spooks — flew into the weapon. I stabbed behind me on instinct, desperate. I whiffed, but the shotgun was loaded now. Swiveling and quickly analyzing the crowd, I found the thickest clump of soldiers and aimed right at their center. I readied Baby for a giant horizontal swing — putting that arm over my shotgun arm and across my chest — and fired.

Just as the shotty's shot spread out, I started my slice. The glowing blue shrapnel dug into four spooks' spectral flesh, dimming some of their glow and making them sink. Baby was right behind — she dug into each of their now much more physical chests and dealt a vicious blow, now working as just a regular sword against them.

The four flew back, giving me a second to collect the billions of thoughts ramming inside my head: *Why are the soldiers completely ignoring Gus? Is there something special about him. Or is it me?*

I waved Baby around. The spooks stared at her, transfixed but still moving towards me.

What the hell did Agatha want from Horst? What was this fuckin' item that he was so desperate to retrieve for her — to the point of reciting its name like a prayer.

My sword split one spook's head in two like an axe chopping wood, Severing him.

Suddenly, wind *blasted* around me, obscuring my hearing. Rain slapped twice as loud, now joined by the rustling and whistling of wind through trees. The chair stopped moving with a mechanical shake.

I was outside the tower. At the highest point in all of Hartsville. Thunder rumbled in greeting, welcoming me to His domain.

The town sprawled in front of me, almost like a diorama from this height — buildings like children's blocks, streets like veins. The small forest surrounding the mansion looked like street-side bushes, waving and snapping with the sharp breeze. The tower's burgundy roof sloped steeply, steep enough that I wouldn't be able to stand on it, especially not with the pelting rain. I'd have to fight on the fuckin' chair.

Spooks moved through the roof, settling around me in a near perfect circle. I'd managed to Sever a few; there were sixteen left, none even slightly deterred by the destruction of some of their buddies.

The soldiers moved in unison, a circle of death closing like a snake on its prey.

C'mon, think!

Their snarling faces came into view through the rain. Some had snouts, others loose-hanging flesh where their noses once were.

What the fuck is the word, Graves!? Something that Agatha was looking for, eighty years ago. Something that she never managed to get because Horst got caught.

Even through the thunder, their growls and gurgles became audible.

Something that the millions of deaths these things would have caused might've earned her... so an item with high esteem in the Other Side.

Lightning flashed nearby, reflecting off the plates drilled into the sides of their heads.

Something she still wants.

The train of thought was constantly interrupted by the

swarming spooks and raucous weather, but I was getting closer. Something *itched* in the back of my skull, and I was too distracted to scratch it.

Then they were on me.

Every monster grabbed a different part of my body. One grabbed my wrist, while another pulled my hair; one grabbed my calf, while another grabbed my arm; one grabbed my inner-thigh, while another dug his fingers into my check—

I screamed.

With a sickening sound, the soldier moved his nails through the flesh of my face like a shovel through dirt. He gripped once his fingers were deep enough inside, then *ripped.* Skin and muscle tore off my face like a Band-Aid. Blood gushed. Iron flowed into my mouth in a red wave. My throat went raw from shouting in pain. The teeth on that side of my jaw went cold, now messily exposed to the outside air.

They didn't stop there.

They punched and tore and ripped until all I could do was raise Baby far above my head, outside the crowd, tip pointing towards the heavens. They looked at her tip even as they beat me to a pulp

What are they so interested in, anyway, I thought, exhausted, head foggy. *Is this why they ignored Gus? Because they wanted Baby?*

And what about Mrs. Garcia? She was possessed by one of these things, but it didn't actually do *anything until... until I pulled out my sword...*

They care so much about her. It's almost like...

Like they're programmed to.

That's it.

I breathed in, air stinging as it rushed through my bloody mouth and tired lungs. Then I screamed as loud as I could.

"CHRONALIUS!"

The soldiers stopped almost immediately.

They backed up and floated there silently, staring at *me* now, instead of Baby. I gasped for breath, raw and bloody and beaten... and so fucking *tired.* It felt like I was holding a semi-truck above me, Baby's weight increasing by the second. I bent my elbow, ready to put her down and—

Lightning struck.

It didn't strike a tree. Or the roof. Or a telephone pole. Or a fuckin' bird.

It struck Baby.

So it struck me.

Pain like nothing I've ever felt squirmed through my body like worms through mud. Every inch of flesh, every follicle of hair, every nerve under my skin was sent through a trash compactor, ground between glass and used needles. The agony was so profound that time slowed to a stop. The spooks around me, now harmless, simply stared at the human lightning rod in front of them. I couldn't move for fear that any disturbance in my body would cause it to collapse into ash. My vision *flooded* with blue, the veins in my eyes snaked visibly across my sight. My scream was raspy and dry.

My heart stopped.

Chapter 20

Coincidences

I was ripped away from the rooftop, my head and hair whipping from the sudden jolt. Rain passed through my glowing, translucent skin. Dazed, I looked behind me... at my own body, frozen with my Blade stretched towards the heavens. As I flew, my body shrunk to a black dot on the horizon, Jenny's mansion soon followed, then the entire town.

I zipped over glistening grass and sleepy towns and snowy lakes — miles and miles in a matter of minutes, all wind and cold and rain unfelt by my ghostly flesh. Forests like tiny gardens, rivers like an ancient's blue veins, splashing through angry clouds like black balls of cotton — until I met a flood of light.

What I thought was the fresh sun was a bustling city, lights of all sorts and colors buzzing along each sky-scraping building, each taller than the next. One dwarfed any structure that I'd come across since entering this realm, its tip dipping into the roiling blackness above it like a quill into ink.

I stopped in front of it.

Droplets pattered against its metal and against the glass windows in which danced humanly silhouettes. I fell downwards suddenly and screamed... until I realized I was already half-dead. *Not much that a plain of concrete can do to me now.*

Dozens of little ants strolled and argued and honked and lived, each a copy of the next, each human life worth an exactly equal amount. They grew, becoming women and men and cars. I flew past them and through the sidewalk as easy as space. Solid earth wasn't enough to stop my careening. And, the further I fell, the more sure I became of my destination.

He'd pulled this shit before. *You can't teach an old dog new tricks*, as they say. And the Reaper is pretty much older than every dog that has ever lived in this realm combined.

I stopped, facing only pure darkness, ancient soil and wriggling critters surrounding me for miles on end.

The Earth rumbled. *Graves*, it said, everywhere and nowhere.

"'Sup." My voice was like a spook's, doubling and echoing.

What have you done this time? Why do I sense your near-demise before midnight?

"It's complicated. Job kinda went haywire on me."

You should not choose death. You have obligations that need fulfilling. Goddess Agatha—

"*Demi*-goddess," I corrected. "Let's not get ahead of ourselves."

... Demi-Goddess Agatha has a right to your life, thus your Blade, if you fail her. And me.

"Oh, so does this mean I get a *second* second chance? Great! I was just about to win that fight, too."

The earth quaked, loud and jarring. *This is no game, Graves. You earned Chronalias as a reward for your conquests, but a conquest in return will rob you of it. Is that what you wish?*

"It won't happen," I said. "Baby was *given* to me. I'd rather give her to my fuckin' *cat* than to Agatha."

The Reaper laughed, like boulders making love. *You still claim that the Blade of Balance was not won through victory and death? Through blood and battle?*

I didn't reply.

The Blade's previous owner died screaming as you smote her. A scream that still echoes through the Other Side — through every realm that can listen. In the Bowels, the demons praise you, yet wonder why you have left them. Far above, near the Gates, those holy creatures curse you with each breath. All speak your name — you have earned that, Graves.

Yet you fled, he quaked. *After reaping her soul so dutifully and snatching Chronalius like a ripe fruit—*

I clenched my fists until each knuckle popped. "Don't you fucking speak of her."

Why not? It was by your hand that your mother perished, not mine. To be sure, I never thought the thirst was in you. Never would have I expected—

"*Shut the fuck up!*" I shouted into the shadows.

A paradox. Only a son of mine could steal such a life, yet no creature I'

d call kin would live among mortals. The voice boomed, chuckling. *Graves, my disappointment, my shame. But you still have potential. I see the souls you send to me, boy. I count each one. You wish to earn my respect, is that it? All it took was a single swing of your sword, and the scream that still resounds throughout the Other Side.*

"I don't give a fuck what you think about me," I snarled. "I won't hear another second of your fucking bullshit. I *know* you killed her. Who else would? My mother was a Warrior of God, and only the great Reaper would benefit from her death."

Benefit? he rumbled, incredulous. *If you were here,*

Graves, you would know your accusations for the air they are. Why do you think I sent Agatha to persecute you? Your lies ring hollow.

"*I didn't fucking kill her,* you bag of wind and bones."

Then prove it, Bastard.

There was a stretch of silence, and ample time to consider my fate — my past, present, and future. The Reaper was a constantly watching force, yet I glared back just as fiercely. I wouldn't let him stand in my way. Not now.

Tell me. If you do not seek my approval, what is it you want? Why do you not return and claim the fruits of your labor? You have nothing to fear from me, in that case.

I stayed silent.

His growl was rocks rolling down a jagged cliffside. *Your mother was secretive too, Graves. There was much even I did not know about her. But she loved. She trusted. Be careful you do not make the same mistakes she did.*

"Are you going to fucking bring me back or not? My body's probably getting real cold."

The Reaper rumbled contemplatively. *We will meet again, Bastard of Death. For your sake, I hope it is not Agatha that sends you back to me.*

Go. Prove your innocence and weakness at once.

He showed me his real voice, his rattling cackle like bones in an iron bowl. An arch of light opened in front of me. Through it wafted the scent of summer — grass and soil, leaves and sweet fruit, saltwater and scratchy sand. Warm wind caressed me, a song wafting along it, begging for my return.

I stared through the warm brightness, listening to the Reaper's laugh and the desperate pleading.

I turned away from the light and shuffled back into the cool, endless darkness.

"*Holy fuck*," I gasped.

All of my strength had returned; I'd essentially gone through a hard reset. Baby was a feather in my grip, still buzzing with electricity. Thunder boomed, lightning flashed, rain slapped, and the frankenspooks wheezed lethargically. They looked at me with their beady eyes, emotionless, waiting for instructions from their new overlord. I grinned at them, then at Baby's radiant tip.

"Fucking *die*," I instructed.

I pushed Baby in front of me, flat side up, then pivoted and spun on my heel.

Blue electricity trailed behind her as she blurred and sliced through the frankenspooks. Baby cut through each like they were made of water, not only bisecting them completely but filling the plates in their heads with enough electricity to make them erupt in a spectral representation of an explosion.

The power of God.

My other foot planted hard on the chair as I stopped my spin. Electricity still snapped around me, lingering in Baby's wake. The frankenspooks each gasped and fell in half.

Before they puffed into mist, the last of Charlie's squad looked at me thankfully, hopeful for their long-awaited rest.

I fell into the chair and let the rain drench me. It washed away the blood and froze the pain as I let my mind wander. This case was done. Finished.

But it wasn't the end of my struggles; I still had Agatha to deal with, and I wasn't a fuckin' *toe* closer to finding her a host. Brightness filled the night sky, but it quickly reverted back to its starless self, staring and looming and... waiting.

I hoped Gus would enjoy the full pay if Agatha turned me into a pile of mush.

After a few minutes of basking in the freezing downpour, I yelled, "Gus! You down there?"

"Yeah!" he hollered back, his voice echoing through the hollow tower. "Uh, how are you doing?"

"Little more well-done than I would've hoped, but breathing. You mind pulling that lever?"

He obliged; the chair lowered slowly, pulling me away from the Lord's judging stare and back into Jennifer's mansion.

"What's got you?" I asked, hopping off the chair and finally back onto solid ground.

"Um," Gus said, stifling more laughs. He was near red in the face from his snickering. "I, uh, like your haircut."

My palm *slapped* loudly as I went to caress my flowing locks. God damn it... er, *damned* it. My five o'clock shadow was gone, too, as were my black eyebrows. I chuckled alongside the chubby medium. "I've always wanted to try the bald look, anyway. More menacing."

I turned my head and peered around the lab — which, all and all, had seen little damage. "Place doesn't look too—"

"*Jesus Christ!*" Gus yelled.

I spun around rapidly, looking for the threat. The room was empty.

"Fuckin' what?" I said, still on alert.

"Your *face*, Graves. What on *Earth happened?*"

I reached up to feel my cheek and nearly yelped as my fingers touched my bare teeth. I grimaced, which probably looked horrifying with half of my face ripped off. "Yikes," I said. "This ain't gonna make getting 'tang much easier."

Gus hesitantly studied the gaping hole. "How haven't you bled out?"

"I guess the lightning strike cauterized all of my wounds. Fancy that."

"You got struck by *lightning!?* Graves, what the *hell* happened up there? Did you figure out the deactivation phrase? What was it?" He waited for a second, then said, "*And how did you survive getting struck by friggin' lighting?*"

"Hey, it's been known to happen."

Gus scoffed. "And what about the passcode?"

I sighed. This wouldn't be an easy story to relay without giving away too much... You know what? Fuck it. I wasn't even sure why I *wasn't* telling Gus all of this shit anyway.

So I told him everything. And I mean *everything.*

Well, not *everything*, actually. I left out the bits containing my... conversation with the Reaper.

I told him about Agatha, and the deal she and the Reaper had made behind my back — y'know the one. I told him that the same demi-goddess had been Horst's other benefactor. That she'd most likely been giving Horst whatever resources he needed to semi-resurrect his super-soldiers. The millions of lives that Horst's monsters would take would have definitely earned Agatha some high esteem within the Other Side.

She'd hoped that boost in political standing would garner some respect from the Reaper, and that he would give her that item she'd been lusting after for so long: my sword, Baby, *Chronalius*. Horst had a big fat boner for Agatha and he wanted her favor. He made it his personal mission to get the sword for her, to the point of programming his soldiers to specifically go for it if they ever saw it.

Failing in that, Agatha hatched a new plan. And here we were.

"He used the sword's name as his passcode," Gus said ponderously. "What, so he could memorize it?"

"I know it was a long shot, but Horst had no reason ever to suspect that anyone would know Baby's name, let alone that she exists. If any other hunter had taken this case, they'd be a big pile of pudding by now." I picked at my face hole. "Plus, the guy was fuckin' *obsessed* with Agatha; her summoning symbol is all over his mansion, his diary is basically at fanfic levels of horniness, and he has a goddamn *statue* of her, for the Reaper's sake."

"Woah." Gus seemed at a loss for words.

"Yeah, woah. Now I've got like an hour before Agatha comes back and tries to rip my head off, and I'm not even *close* to finding a host for her."

"I'm still kinda confused about that part. If she wants your sword so bad, why wouldn't she just come and kill you anyway?"

"I think her and the Reaper have a kind of compromise. My sword would let her come to our realm in the flesh and do some *real* fuckin' damage; she wouldn't be beholden to any of the Other Side's laws. The Reaper isn't exactly *against* that, but he's not for it, either. I think he offered the compromise: She can kill me and claim Baby if she wants, but only *after* I fail to give her another way to come here and wreak havoc, i.e., a host."

"Why you? I mean, a *goddess*. And the *Reaper*. How the heck did you tied up with *them?*"

"*Demi*-goddess, first of all." I frowned. "And it's a sorta punishment for... something that happened in the past. Something they think I did. I've had a while to settle the score on that front, but I guess the Reaper got tired of waiting."

"Huh," Gus grunted. "What's with the 'a more wicked heart than you' stuff?"

"It's a way of having me prove my innocence. The crime I'm accused of is... serious — a crime even the *Reaper* may not have the strength to commit, though I have my suspicions. If I can find someone more fucked up than me for Agatha, it would show that I'm guiltless."

"And... you are?"

"Yes. But it still won't be easy to find someone who fits the bill, if you get me."

He nodded and rubbed his chin. "Do we have any leads?"

"*We?*" I scoffed. "Alright, kid, this time it's really got nothing to do with you. I just thought you oughta know what happened here and why, but I'll take my own affairs from here."

He said nothing, yet he remained contemplative, a detective stubbornly attached to his case.

Gus' confidence issue had been wiped away like shit from my stinking asshole.

"This can't all be a coincidence, right?" he asked. "I mean, you've got a deal with this demi-goddess from Hell, then the next case you take has to do with something she was *directly involved in*?"

"Yes," I replied flatly. "It *can* all be a coincidence. If you've got some all-connecting thread in mind, be my fuckin' guest."

He shook his head and scrunched up his eyebrows in thought. "And what about me?"

I flinched. "What *about* you?"

"Why was *I* involved? You said it yourself yesterday: This and Mallery's cases feel orchestrated to attract *your* attention, but also *mine.*"

"That's still a coincidence, kid," I sighed. "I just went to Mallery's because I had to pay Josephi off, and he'd dropped the case right in my lap. *You* showed up because Josephi told you to..."

Gus' face lit up.

While mine dipped into a black tar of rage.

Who had been involved in *both* of these cases, other than me and Gus? Who did I owe this debt to in the first place?

Who'd swindled me in the past, effectively enslaving me to his will?

Who had known that I needed a host for Agatha, despite me never so much as *mentioning* the demi-goddess?

I'll tell you who: the guy who was about to get sliced and fucking diced like a three-inch cut of Italian sausage.

Chapter 21

Fear

"Little bastard son of a..." I mumbled as I walked through the dark hallway, back towards the spiral staircase.

"Graves!" Gus called after me.

"Rip the little fucker's head off, that's what I'll do. Limp dick ass—"

"Graves! Where are you going? What's the plan?"

I practically exploded through the secret passage door, then went thundering down the stairs. "Thinks he can play me? Thinks Imma fuckin' idiot? I'll show him. And that ghost bitch, too." My boots squeaked on the polished marble. "Play the douchebag's throat like a bagpipe."

I threw open the mansion's front door with all my might. Moonlight filtered through the stained glass set into the door's windows, creating a mystical dance on the floor around me. Then it shattered as it slammed against the wall, shards tinkling along the black marble.

"Graves! Think! That demi-goddess — Agatha — will probably defend Josephi. We need a plan! You can't just rush in and—"

"Oh, I *gotta* fuckin' plan," I growled, turning around. "It's called the 'rush in and kill everything in fucking sight' plan. What do you think? Roll off the tongue?"

"We can't—"

"Yeah, you're right. *We* can't do shit. *I* can. Pack it up,

Gus. All you'll do is get yourself fuckin' killed. We're dealing with god-level shit here. Go home."

His pale face curdled, but I turned away and continued striding. I'd been too pissed to check the time, but I guessed that it was around eleven, which gave me an hour to...

To do what? Kill Josephi? Then what?

I don't know, man. But the fury bubbling inside me at that moment was so *vicious* — so *acidic* — that nothing could stand between me and throttling that little weasel like a sock on my cock.

Gus huffed and puffed behind me. "Graves! I'm coming too!"

"Gus, if I have to fucking knock you out—"

"How are you gonna get there? Huh? It's the middle of the night!"

My nose wrinkled as I grimaced. The night's cold air brushed against my bared teeth and gums, pinching my nerves. Fire rose inside my stomach.

Fucking Gus God shit fuck Josephi, I thought.

Then I slammed my foot onto the ground and roared into the night sky, rain splattering against my tongue and eyes as they opened wide. I roared until my lungs emptied like balloons. My throat felt like it was doused in gasoline.

And suddenly, I felt the best I had in days, every inch of toxic fury leaking through my quivering jowls with my bestial roar.

I stopped, gasping for breath. A warmth filled me — a confidence, a desire to live.

A focused need to *kill*.

Gus walked up to me and put his hand on my shoulder. "Let's get this asshole."

I inhaled, taking in the night air. It smelled of dirt and rain and life.

Wordlessly, I climbed into Gus' van.

As he drove, I planned.

I pictured Josephi's intestines spelling my name on the front windows of his office.

Or me pulling his eyes right from their sockets, then stabbing a little plastic sword through them and sticking them in a pair of martinis.

Here's a good one: A big Josephi-skin rug to decorate my log cabin. I imagined me and a lovely lady cuddling up on Josephi's cold flesh, his eternal scream complimenting my explosive climax.

But these dreams rang hollow. I didn't *know* what I was gonna do when we got to Josephi's flat. What if Agatha *did* show up?

I'd have to fight her.

Gus might think I'm the bee's knees — and I agree — but I was pretty sure that fight would end with me in pieces.

We parked nearby Josephi's place. I marched towards his door, noting that the lights inside were on, and readied myself for a proper break-in.

Before I could slam my shoulder through his door, Gus whispered, "*Wait.*"

I did, looking at him questioningly. He pointed at his ear, so I put mine up to the door and listened.

"There's just no way," Josephi said, his voice flowing and practiced. "How could Graves survive that? Didn't you say that those monsters were practically indestructible?"

"They were *supposed* to be," a feminine voice hissed.

Agatha.

"Well, they weren't," Josephi snapped back. "In fact, they were *very* destructible."

"If you hadn't sent the *smart one* along with Graves, the Bastard would have died right then and there. Chronalius would be mine... and you would have all the power a mortal can dream of."

"That 'smart one' was your *host*. The very second you said Graves had been killed, we could've gone and grabbed the kid. The Union would've thought he died right alongside Graves, and you would've had a fresh, free vessel."

"Even *with* the mortal's help, Graves should have perished just from lack of warning. But, out of your disgusting cowardice, you *informed* him that Erick Horst still lived!" Agatha's tone dripped with sizzling acid. "And now I've been Marked, because I had to clean up *your* mess."

"Hey, Graves is a monster; I don't trust the guy not to murder me, no matter what you say. He makes you look like a kitten."

"I should *kill* you for the way you speak to me!" Agatha shrieked.

"Try it, toots. You know the Reaper would be on you in an instant if you broke a Favor like that, let alone killed a mortal."

I heard her growl and grunt in effort. The wall next to me and Gus exploded outwards, sheetrock and dust billowing. One of Josephi's larger awards was sitting on the street outside after the debris had faded.

"Hey!" Josephi yelled. "That cost money, you know!"

"One more word," Agatha snarled, "and I will—"

"Ladies, ladies!" I said, walking through the hole in the wall. "The man of the hour is *right here*. Enough of the bickering! Let's solve this like rational adults, huh?"

I smiled wolfishly at Josephi — who was at a complete loss for words, practically pissing himself — and quickly drew Baby.

"Oh, *Christ*," Josephi yelped. He jumped behind Agatha's floating body, hands over his head and quaking. "Graves, dis ain't what it looks like. I was... uh... *trickin'* her, see? I had ya back, Graves! Haven't I always!?"

"Silence, you *oaf*," Agatha spat.

Josephi continued pleading. "Please, Graves! Don't kill me! I didn't—"

"*Shut the fuck up,*" I snapped, voice cracking like thunder. "Josephi, there is not a single fucking thing on the face of this Earth that will keep me from killing you. Not the police. Not the Union. Not even this dumb ghost bitch right here. Beg and plead all you want. Your life ends tonight."

He started bawling. I basked in that.

Agatha's bubbling giggle cascaded in front of me. "Strong words for a man who is destined to perish, Graves," she cackled. "Or have you brought me some poor, wicked fool to possess?"

I glared at her.

"You haven't? How sad. Then maybe you'd like to cut your time short, hm? Just end your suffering? It looks like you may have already had your fill." She eyed the hole in my cheek. Her confident, tinkling laughter made me rethink certain decisions.

I took a few deep breaths and closed my eyes

In all my life, there have been precious few truths: Pabst is piss, sex is bliss, and there's very little I can't solve with my sword and my shotgun. This might be pushing that last truth to its limits, but everyone has to have faith in something, right?

With my eyes still closed, I positioned Baby in front of me and put my other arm behind my back, a direct challenge to Agatha.

I opened my eyes.

Agatha threw her head back and *wailed.*

"Finally!"

Darkness seemed to bend *towards* her, shadows inverted. Slabs of meat fell from her face, revealing that haunting purple skull. Her eyes pierced me like needles. A howl escaped her skeletal jaw, like a wolf on the hunt.

This was it.

"Dat's him!" Josephi said, pointing towards the gaping hole behind me. "Dat's ya host, Agatha! You take his body and he'll take all ya hits! No point in dyin' when tubby can do it for ya, right?"

Agatha's skull clacked as she turned her gaze away from me and focused every ounce of hatred, desire, determination, anger, and hunger...

On Gus.

"Me...?" he said.

"Yeah, youse." Josephi coughed out a laugh. "Go on, Agatha. You take dis guy's body, we take Graves out, den you give me my powers — den I make some *money!"*

I grimaced. If Agatha killed me and claimed Baby, not only would she be free to kill anytime she wanted — one of her many rights as the wielder of the Blade of Balance — she'd have Gus as a secondary suit of fleshy armor. Something to take a few hits for her and toss away like a foil wrapper. Really not that essential. It was just a way for Josephi to earn some extra good boy points from Agatha.

Gus wasn't a person to her. He was the toy in a Happy Meal.

"I... I..." Gus stammered.

"Agatha," I said warningly, "the kid has nothing to do with this. You've got no fuckin' reason to possess him. If you get Baby, what the hell are you gonna do with Gus? What's it matter?"

Her teeth clacked as she laughed. “Aw, Graves. Are you telling me you care for the boy? That is a first. I didn’t think ‘caring’ had any place within your emotional index. That was really the last trait of yours I’d admired, in fact.” A thick violet tongue came out of her bared mouth and licked the front of her teeth, making sickening slurping noises. “This newfound heart of yours will make each bite of your soul that much more... *juicy*. It will pop like an orange between my jaws.” Her fiery eyes swished back over to Gus. “But I’ll start with you, little man.”

You... you can’t,” Gus said. “I won’t—”

“I plan to jump into your mind and scramble it, like ice into slurry, if only to draw some sort of reaction from Graves before I kill him.” She cackled. “You may run if you like. The result will come no slower — a severing of all consciousness from your body, a complete loss of control before you ultimately perish in stretched mental anguish.” Her eyes went feral, pupils shrinking to green pinpricks. “Graves’ misery will be worth every second I have to spend in your flabby body. Take pride in that!” she finished with a shriek, then sped towards Gus with claws outstretched.

Time slowed.

Agatha had zipped in front of me. Her metallic skull was clacking and shaking with twisted glee. She hadn’t even bothered summoning her stupid sword. Not yet, at least.

Gus’ face showed almost no emotion. He stood, chubby and unsuspecting, waiting to be devoured inside and out by this being of comparatively incalculable power. As I looked at his innocent, vulnerable expression — chubby cheeks jiggling, blue eyes wide, hands clenched with nerves — something occurred to me.

Agatha was right.

Ever since I’d left the Other Side, I had little room in my

mind for anything but myself and my goals (and Hans). I was so desperate for revenge I hadn't even considered what else I'd find on *this* side. After I came to live in the realm of mortals, I immediately joined the Union and started hunting down spooks. Yeah, I'd met Aubrey through work, but I could hardly call her my friend. Everyone else I hardly thought twice about.

Gus, though... Gus had had my back. He'd gone out of his way to fight alongside me, not just because he wanted to "prove himself" or whatever, but because he thought I'd have a legitimately better chance of surviving if he was there. It wasn't until afterwards that I saw how right he was. All in all, he was a genuinely good dude. He had his own goals and aspirations, his own troubles and flaws. I didn't love the guy or anything — I still didn't really *like* anyone on this side — but he'd kinda turned my expectations topsy-turvy. He was more than just a sack of bones and meat, of frivolous emotions and impulses. Yeah, he was annoying and desperate for approval and bad at coming up with names, but...

I didn't want him to die. I cared.

Fuck me, it hurt to admit that.

But imagining his little brain pureed like a vegan's midnight snack was even less pleasant.

Crazed laughter came from near where Agatha had been. Josephi was clapping his hands and jumping up and down, gleeful, dollar signs already sparkling in front of him.

I knew I shoulda killed that little fuckin' freak when I had the chance.

The only important person in Josephi's life was the man himself. All the guy did was fuck people over. Hell, his entire career was *based* around it. *Answers From the Other Side* preyed on grieving family members and friends — those people who needed *some* closure. Josephi hadn't helped a single person during his entire career at the Union, either. All he did was take their cases, then pass them out to other, actually *qualified* hunters while taking a cut of the pay. The scumbag had found every way to cheat and worm his way to the top.

He'd ruined countless lives and livelihoods, and made a fat load of cash while doing it. Gus, Emily, Jessie, even fucking me — no one was safe from the scumbag. Now here he was sacrificing a *teenager* to a demi-goddess from Hell. And for what? To get some powers that would make his act on TV more convincing? Just to earn some extra cash? Everything and everyone around Josephi had a price, which was solely based on how much selling them would inconvenience him in the long run.

I realized that Josephi was one of the worst, scummiest, dirtiest, piece-of-shittiest pieces of shit I'd ever met.

I mean, Christ, I thought, *the fucker's even worse than me...*

Time went back to normal.

"Hold the *fuck* up, bitch," I said.

Agatha stopped on a dime, then spun in the air and faced me. "Your time will come soon enough, Bastard. Or are you—"

"Shut up," I said. "Neither me nor the kid are dying tonight. In fact, Josephi, you might be glad to hear that *no one* is gonna have a playdate with the Old Man downstairs."

"What are youse talkin' about?" Josephi asked.

"*Silence*," Agatha hissed. "This idiot is lying. He has nothing. He simply doesn't want his little pet to die. Isn't that right, Bastard?"

I stared at her, pointedly avoiding looking at Gus. "As much as I hate to admit it," I said, "you're right, Agatha. I don't want Gus to die. He doesn't deserve it. He might be the only one in this room who doesn't."

This was the first time the noisy, boney whore didn't have anything to say.

"But that's not why I stopped you." I smiled. "I just didn't want you to spoil your appetite."

She rolled her eyes. "Just say what you mean, fool."

"Well, I don't want to *inconvenience* you or nothin', but I've got a ready and less than willing host all fluffed and lubed up for your pleasure."

Her laugh rang a little less solid, this time. "You truly think you can bluff your way out of this? You don't even have enough—"

"Gus, my boy, what time is it?"

Gus flinched, jolting out of his state of shock. "Uh, it's 11:56," he mumbled.

"You see, Agatha? Plenty of time for you to waltz your plump little ass across the room and hop right into..." I pantomimed holding a microphone up to my mouth, then waved my hand exaggeratedly towards Josephi, "your brand-new car!"

"WHAT!?" Josephi practically leaped and gripped onto the ceiling like a cat. "What duh *hell* do youse—"

"Graves," Agatha said calmly. Suddenly, every ounce of panic and energy flooded out of the room. She said my name with such confidence that Josephi visibly calmed, as if whatever she was about to proclaim would undoubtedly save his festering ass. Her face was covered in spotless pale flesh once again. "I have met hundreds of slimy, irredeemable individuals in my millennia of life." A small, cute smile curled on her face. "But rarely have I met one that reaches *your* level. Your level of selfishness. Greed. She was adored by all — a literal *saint* — yet you could not let her wield such power when it could so easily be yours. You could not live as *just* the Reaper's bastard. You needed Chronalius, lest you be outclassed by the others within the Bowels.

"How could you possibly think that this simple conman — this bumbling *buffoon* — could overcome *your* level of wickedness, Graves? He is little more than a swindler of fools, like so many thousands of sniveling thieves before him, while *you* slaughtered a Warrior of God. Someone whose sole purpose was to sustain peace and uphold justice. Your own mother."

Her smile faded. She stared at me, waiting for a response, sure that she wasn't gonna get one.

"It doesn't matter what you think, Agatha," I said. "It matters what *I* think. And I think that Josephi is a... a worse person than I am."

"How can you be so sure?" Agatha sneered.

"'Cause I don't think the dweeb back there," I nodded towards Gus, who looked confused, "deserves to die. I'd rather he didn't. You were right, Agatha." I clenched my jaw. "I fuckin' *care.*

"Meanwhile, Josephi saw an insecure, amateur hunter and decided to monetize not just his desperation for validation, but his *death.*"

Agatha narrowed her eyes. "Perhaps. But you killed your own *mother,* Graves, just for material gain. Even if you claim otherwise, the truth reveals itself before our very eyes."

"Does it?" I spat back at her. "If you're so confident, try to kill me and take my sword. I'm sure it's past midnight now, so if Josephi isn't an adequate host, the Reaper won't stop you. C'mon, bitch. Come at me. See what the fuck happens."

Her fists shook with fury, but she didn't move.

"The Reaper might not know the truth of what happened to my mother, but he knows emotion — he knows the fear of death, the confidence of life, the acceptance of an end — and he'll recognize my conviction." I rushed towards her, Baby in my grip. She flinched back, growling, but I stopped just in front of her. I looked up into her eyes and sneered. "Now stop wasting my fuckin' time, and either try something on me or possess that little fucker and get the hell outta my face."

I said this with the utmost confidence, but one fact still clung to the back of my mind like a kidney stone: After Agatha possessed Josephi, she'd still be here in the flesh, relatively clear to do whatever she wants with her power and her sword.

That wouldn't normally be a problem, but because I was the one who *gave* her the host, I couldn't do shit to stop her. It'd be up to the rest of the Union to send Agatha packing, and even the entire organization and its members may not have been equipped enough.

But, as I looked over and studied Josephi — quaking in his boots and sniveling like a child, staring at me as if I were some feral beast — I got an idea.

"Well!?" I roared at Agatha.

She rattled with rage, then howled and shrieked towards the sky.

"*Damn you, Bastard of Death!* I *will* kill you. Once I possess this fool, I will kill everyone around you — everyone in this pathetic, little town — starting with the fat boy. I will kill until your military comes and riddles his body with bullets, then I will return to the Other Side and begin planning for your demise. You will *not* escape me!"

"Try me, bitch. I'll be waiting."

She shrieked again, then suddenly flew at Josephi. He screamed and whimpered, tears flying from his face.

"No-no, Agatha! Please! Wese had a deal! You don't have to do dis! I—" Then she was inside him.

Josephi's eyes widened, rolling all the way back into his

skull. His mouth opened wider than should be humanly possible; his jaw cracked and unhinged. Agatha flew into his maw like a flood of water. Josephi shook and gagged and choked as she did. Finally, her spectral body disappeared inside of him. His mouth stayed open, a shrill squeaking stemming from the back of his throat.

His eyes rolled forward, now glowing purple with piercing green pupils. His jaw slammed closed with a clack, and Agatha laughed behind the mask. "He doesn't feel as awful as I would have thought," she said.

"Yeah, the guy's fit," I replied, chuckling right alongside her.

"Why do you laugh, Graves? Your little pet is about to die by my hand. I will drench you in his—"

"Woah, woah. Let's not get ahead of ourselves, Josephi. I don't think we're through talking yet."

"Josephi...? Graves, stop your games for once. Humor cannot mask your fear. Not when—"

"Josephi," I said, glaring at her. "Shut the fuck up. Right now."

Her mouth closed instantly. Agatha's eyebrows shot up in surprise. She tried to say something else, but it came out as mumbles through her sealed lips.

Finally, she forced her jaw open. "What... what have you done, Bastard? Why do I not have full control of this body?"

Beads of sweat streamed down her cheek. I remembered the small gleams of Beefboy's humanity that'd shined through his eyes, even *after* he'd been possessed. His will was *almost* strong enough, his emotions *almost* powerful enough.

"Fear is a powerful weapon," I said through my smile. "Josephi, you know that I'll kill you if you step even a *hair* out of line, right?"

Agatha gave no reaction.

"*Fucking answer me!*" I roared.

Her head nodded rapidly. "W-w-what i-is h-h-happening," Agatha said as her face moved up and down repeatedly. She squeezed the sides of her head, forcing the gesture to stop.

"Looks like you're renting a duplex, not a studio. Josephi's still in there with you, and he's *terrified*."

Tears formed in the corners of their eyes. "You *idiot*," Agatha's voice shrieked. "He cannot kill me, so neither can he kill *you*. You are completely—"

"It's not true!" Josephi said, overlapping Agatha's sweet tones. "Graves'll slaughter me like a pig! I knows it! He's always been waitin' too, and now's his chance!"

"No! He can't!" they replied to themselves.

I bellowed laughter at them. "Oh *man,* this is rich! Josephi, you're so piss scared of me that the *literal* god inside of you isn't enough to strengthen your nerve!" I laughed until a tear streamed down my cheek.

"Graves, this was not in the agreement," Agatha said.

"Yeah, but it wasn't *not* in the agreement, neither." I grinned. "Hey, Josephi."

"Whuh... what is it?" came Josephi's timid voice.

"If you don't leave town *right fucking* now, I swear to God I'll stick this sword so far down your fucking throat you'll have to go on a low-iron diet for the rest of your life."

He stared at me for a minute, expression flickering between terrified and hateful.

"Gra... Graves, you cannot escape me—"

"Five," I said.

"I will gut you like—"

"Four."

"Not even the Reaper could save—"

"Three." I yawned exaggeratedly and checked my nails.

"You'll be begging for—"

"Tuh-whoooo," I sang.

"I... I'm not scared of you."

Baby pulsing with hunger in my fist, I took a lunge towards them. "One," I whispered, inches away from Josephi's face.

They bolted.

And I mean fuckin' *bolted.*

Josephi stumbled away from me and fell over himself. He went for the door, but slammed into it, forgetting that it was locked. His head swiveled, searching for an escape route. He saw the massive hole in his wall, then he sprinted through it and passed Gus, whimpers echoing through the empty night.

I vaguely heard him and Agatha bickering as they ran — Josephi steadfast on fleeing, Agatha furious yet helpless. She would be trapped with that conniving rat until she either drove him insane or he died of old age, after a lifetime of ranting about and arguing with the demi-goddess stuck in his head. Either way, it would be fuckin' hilarious.

Me and Gus shared a look, then we laughed — him nervously, me gripping my stomach and bellowing towards the black sky.

"*Keep fucking running, Josephi! Don't look back! Because I'll be there! Always!*"

Chapter 22

Until Death

So, I was just a *toy* to that lady?" Gus asked as we drove through the sleeping Hartsville, towards the forest that surrounded it. The rain had lightened; soft sprinkles fell on his windshield as we moved. The moon caressed the town, basking its buildings in dim light and pushing away their hungry shadows.

"More or less," I said, peacefully observing the scenery.

Gus frowned and looked at his hands, sulking.

"Don't take it personal, kid. Trust me when I say you were *way* out of your league in that room."

"And I survived," he mumbled, looking back at the road.

"And you survived," I agreed.

We drove into the shadow-drenched forest, moonlight peeking here and there, speckling the terrain with color.

"What's your plan now?" Gus asked.

"Same that it's always been: Kill some spooks, make some dough, get some ass."

"And that's it?"

I went silent. Gus hadn't pushed for much info these past two days; he knew the boundaries. Why now?

He'd seen something he couldn't explain. He knew about the Other Side, of course — everyone in the Union did; the spooks had to go *somewhere*. But, Gus hadn't known much about it. He didn't know that *gods* existed — or at least that they lived in a very tangible and very real place. He realized that, now that he was a professional hunter, he'd be pretty close to *directly* interacting with a place he knew next to nothing about. Gus wanted answers.

And I wasn't about to give them.

"And that's it," I replied,

I directed Gus off the beaten path, towards my shack.

"And you?" I asked. "You gotta plan?"

"Same thing, I guess. Minus the ass."

I chuckled. "And what about that girl?"

"Jessie? I don't know." He bit his lip. "They're pretty mad about me taking a case without them, I think."

"Didn't they do the same?"

"Well... yeah. But that was to pay Josephi, I guess. The Garcias' case was at least..."

"Sounds like they have some 'splainin to do."

"What do you mean?"

"I mean *ask* them why they took a case without you."

"It's not that simple. Em doesn't like to talk; she was never a team player. I don't think I could really make her budge."

"*You* don't?" I said. "The same you that captured the soul of *two* Nazi super-soldier ghosts, fought off a horde of the same fuckers, and stared down an ancient demi-goddess from Hell?" I slapped my knee and gestured towards myself. "The same you that stood up against *me*? Don't kid yourself, bucko. And don't forget *why* those girls fucked up that case in the first place."

He beamed, then pulled to the front of my shack. I got out, turned, and reached out and shook his hand.

"Gus. 70/30."

"Wha... Really?"

"Really. Hell, with the work you put in maybe that should be *flipped*."

He smiled, surprised. "You mean that?"

"Well, yeah, it *should*," I said, chuckling. "But it won't be. Go collect the dough from Jennifer ASAP and send me my cut."

The smile remained plastered on his face as he drove off.

I couldn't sleep, so I spent the next few hours cleaning my shack.

And it took every one of those fuckin' hours.

There were dead things around everywhere, plenty of empty beer cans, food wrappers, more dead things I couldn't even identify, and some *Hans'* brand chocolate bars left here and there.

I spent a good chunk of the time organizing my armory. I had used a nice slice of my shells the past few days, so I'd have to make a visit to my supplier. But that could wait.

For now, I focused on cleaning every speck of blood off of Baby's blade. I even applied some leather-cleaner and special scents to her hilt. She purred thankfully as I did. Beautiful and gleaming, I put Baby on her mantle so she could rest up for the next case.

After the cleaning was done, I did some self-maintenance.

Fuck me, did I need that.

I lotioned up my newly-bald scalp, hands scraping against short fuzz. I took a few showers, soaping up parts that hadn't seen the light of day in too long.

Oh, and if *you* think shaving's inconvenient, try doing it around a gaping hole in your fuckin' face. You'll never get used to the taste of shaving cream.

Feeling good and looking better — the sun now rising — I did the thing I'd been avoiding ever since fleeing the Bowels: I went grocery shopping.

I realized that because my healing properties were based

on how much I ate, maybe I should have a little bit more than eggs and beer at home. I didn't get kale or anything — I'm still not a fuckin' health nut — but I'm sure one of the 28 frozen pizzas I bought had olives on it. So I was on my way.

Finally, I made myself a big, fat meal, cracked open one of my favorite dark beers, and feasted with Hans curled next to me, trying not to let anything spill out of the face hole.

I belched in triumph as I finished, then went into the bathroom to see how my face was doing.

The hole was still there and didn't show signs of shrinking. It'd been too long since it was torn open. Shit. I was afraid of that.

Guess that's another problem for later.

One afternoon, as I drank and watched TV with Hans, my phone rang for the first time in days.

"Graves, the Extra-whatever shitternator," I said as I popped open a new beer.

"Charming," came Aubrey's gravely yet high-pitched voice.

"What's up, babe. Little early for a booty call, don't ya think?"

"Fucking pig," she mumbled. Then, louder, she said, "I went and did some investigating at Jennifer's mansion after your call and found some, uh, laboratories... I think. Care to explain?"

"Not really."

I chuckled internally as she growled and braced herself.

"Graves," she said through gritted teeth.

"Oh, alright. Look up 'Erick Horst.' He was the original owner of that mansion — a Nazi first, scientist second, and paranormal-enthusiast third. Those labs were never discovered, so if you're gonna find your big break, it'll be down there."

"Okay. Oh, there was also a giant naked man in the lab at the top of one of the towers. He had fallen down a giant ladder and banged his head pretty bad."

"Shit. Forgot about him. He dead?"

"Your compassion is inspiring," she said. "No, he's alive. But his memory is all but gone. I sent him to the hospital.

"Speaking of, Jennifer asked me to relay a message: 'Come and see me, Mr. Graves. I have an extra reward for you.'"

"*Boy-yo-yoing!*" I shouted. "Thar she blows, cap'n! Ass ahoy!"

"Christ, you're pathetic," Aubrey groaned.

"Don't be jealous, sweety. There's plenty of Graves to go—"

"Just shut the hell up, Graves. I'm going to go check out these labs. Hopefully get my fucking career back. Stay out of trouble, or I'll be there."

"It's a date."

A few days after that, my bank account was filled with Jennifer Nee's money. I was excited to have the extra dough, but it was a little less satisfying without being able to shove it in Josephi's face. I bought ten more six-packs to help me get over it.

Later, I received another chunk of change directly from the Union. The deposit was labelled *Mallery's*, which gave me an itch in my belly.

That never got wrapped up, I realized. *Won't reflect well with the Union, especially if the old bird rats on me.*

I made a few calls, then trudged my way to Mallery's house that afternoon, money on the mind and a twist to my mouth. The construction crew had already arrived, and a group of guys were speaking with the old bird on her porch. She seemed dumbstruck, staring at the workers with watery eyes.

Her voice came into my hearing as I neared: “And the bill? I don’t imagine that I can afford such a task…”

“Taken care of, Ma’am,” one worker answered. “Though the benefactor decided to remain anonymous.”

Mallery sniffed… then her gaze fell on me, standing by her gate. With a lingering look, she turned and went inside. I followed.

“You destroyed my home… and are using my *own* money to rebuild it,” Mallery said as we reached her thrashed kitchen, “but I suppose I am grateful.”

I sputtered. “Lady, I’m just here to make sure you don’t say a word of this to the Union. As long as you keep that wrinkly trap shut, we’re all out of problems.”

She raised an eyebrow, but didn’t push.

A brightness shined behind me, a sudden spotlight into the dreary kitchen. From it descended an old man, portly and with an impressive mustache. He looked at Mallery with glowing blue eyes. “My Mallery,” he groaned.

“Hick... Hickory,” she gasped, hand to her bony chest.

“Look what these boys have done to our house, my love.”

Mallery’s expression turned sour. “I knew I couldn’t trust them, these hunters… but it’s being fixed. I just hope it can look as it did during those final years…”

“Does it matter?” Hickory asked. “Are you happy, Mallery?”

A tear pooled, released, and fell down her wrinkled cheek. “I am, Hickory. Seeing you… Oh... I am.”

The old man’s mustache raised. “Then so am I.” Hickory gave his wife one last longing look, then closed his eyes and faced the beam of light. Bit by bit, he faded away, smiling all the while.

Mallery smiled just as wide, despite the copious tears falling onto her lap.

"Huh," I said.

That night I dreamed of Jenny Nee's fat knockers wrapped around my ding-dong. I don't know if I believe in the Christian version of Heaven, but if it doesn't look like that I don't wanna go there.

I dreamed those incredible dreams right until everything went black. The room, Jennifer, and her big ol' mammary glands vanished in the blink of an eye.

Then the Reaper came a-knockin', entering my dream as if it were his home.

Graves, he rumbled through the darkness.

"What do you want, you old biddy? Last time I looked your titties didn't even come close to Jenny's. B-cups, at best."

I had not expected that you would still draw breath.

"Takes more than a bunch of dumb ghosts and a dumber demi-goddess to take me out, dumb-dumb."

My hearing shook with his laughter. *Perhaps. Know that I never sought to kill you, nor do I attempt to stop whatever threat comes for you. I am mostly ambivalent about your life, but I am curious to see what my seed can accomplish. What is it you are hoping to find up there, Graves? Why do you do my job for me?*

"Frankly?" I said, crossing my legs and lounging, suspended in the darkness. "It's 'cause you fuckin' suck at it."

Excuse me?

"Do you realize that there is an entire organization dedicated to cleaning up after you? The Union was created to deal with wayward spirits, spirits that *you* should be taking care of, not mortals."

Those spirits are lost. There is nothing I can do for them. My duty is to bring death to those whose time has expired.

"Keep telling yourself that," I spat. "*I'll* keep mopping up your mistakes."

You claim you want to Sever these lost dead in some sort of quest for justice?

"I could give two shits about justice, or whether or not some dead guy has closure." That... had a little less truth to it than it may have a few days prior.

What, then? Graves, I will not believe that you left us simply to earn meaningless riches — in a realm you are not even native to.

I grinned at the never-ending expanse of shadow. "I Sever them to prove that I'm *better* than you, Reaper."

His laughter returned. *You are saying this is all an act of childish rebellion? A stance against your father and all he represents?*

"Tell me," I said calmly, "what do you think those in the Other Side and elsewhere will say when they see how sloppily you've handled things in this realm? Do you think they'll be happy?" My smile widened. "Or do you think they'll look for your replacement? Maybe someone who has proven he has what it takes to *actually* flood the Spectral Plain with souls?

"I am your next of kin, after all."

Suddenly, blazing red flooded my vision. I squinted through it, trying to keep my face expressionless. Fire flicked and roiled in front of me in a gigantic ball of heat. A hooded, black skull burst from the center of it, twelve feet tall. Flame spiraled and wormed through its sockets and rattling teeth. Small spikes of bone ran from between its eyes to the back of its head.

I noticed, with a small grin, a small indent on the skull's right temple. Apparently, I'd hit him hard enough to scar.

"Boy, you play with fire," the Reaper said, his voice demonic and shrill. "You have no scope. No *idea* what forces you toy with. I could

Sever your soul before you could so much as *blink*."

"But you won't, Reaper. Even you have to play by the rules. You said it yourself a few days ago: It's not my time. I proved my innocence... but you're not so safe. So why don't you crawl back into your pit and let a real man do his work."

His charred jaw cracked open as he shrieked. Fire swirled out in a solid bar, coming straight towards me. "How long will you continue this foolishness? *I did not kill your mother.*"

"Maybe not, but *someone* did. And I'll find out who if I have to stick a fucking crowbar through your black teeth and *pry* them out myself."

"*Bastard of Death*," he cackled, despite the flame spouting out of his mouth. "You are not worthy of that title! Not even my *bastard* would be foolish enough to challenge me! You will *die* for this insolence, Graves. I control death and all that comes with it; you don't think I can place your time wherever I wish? Watch your back, Bastard, for my eyes will never leave it."

"What's up with everyone and my ass?" I asked, rolling my eyes and sticking my butt out. "It's not *that* nice, is it?"

Flame engulfed me, digging under my flesh and boiling me from the inside out. My eyes melted, nails charred, teeth popped like popcorn. My howl of extreme agony mixed well with my tear-jerking, manic laughter.

If you didn't realize: The Grim Reaper really can't take a joke.

The End